VAMPIRE HEIR

SCORNED BY BLOOD, BOOK ONE

HEATHER RENEE

ISBN: 979-8495482661

Line Editing and Proofing: Jamie from Holmes Edits

Cover: Covers by Juan

Character Art: @kalynne_art on Instagram

CONTENTS

DEDICATION

*To the women of the world who choose to lift others up
instead of tearing them down.
Keep kicking ass.*

PROLOGUE

Seven years ago

I STOOD FROZEN IN HORROR, HIDING IN THE TREES AT OUR property line, and helpless to do anything as I watched the air be choked from my mother. My heart pounded so rapidly, I thought I would pass out, but there would be no reprieve from what I was witnessing.

Five men stood outside of my house, but one of them held my attention the most. He was dressed in dark clothes with a significant widow's peak and holding my mother by her neck. He leaned in and kissed her just above her collarbone, a gesture I didn't understand.

She screamed, but the sound only lasted seconds until her arms fell limp at her sides. He dropped her onto the ground before joining the other four behind him. They laughed and cheered as each of them sped away at impossible speeds opposite to where I was crouched behind the brush.

I didn't understand what I had seen. This had to be a nightmare I could wake up from.

Dread filled my chest as I forced myself to take the heavy steps toward the house. I'd only been gone ten minutes. Long enough to make the short walk to the store for the milk we needed to finish dinner. Milk that had been dropped to the ground when I first heard my mother's screams.

Tears spilled from my eyes as my mother came into view. My hands trembled as I bent over her prone body, grabbing her shirt to turn her over. Blood coated my fingers where I held her, making my stomach churn, and it was my mother's lifeless eyes that caused sobs to rip from deep inside me.

"No, no, no," I repeated over and over when no other words came to me.

I laid next to her on the cold wet ground, unable to fathom a world without my mother. She was the light that led our family. She couldn't truly be gone. It was too soon. I wasn't ready to live without her.

Our front door creaked, reminding me that my brother and father had also been home, but neither of them had come out of the house yet.

I needed to get up and find them. I needed to know what my heart was already telling me, but I wasn't ready to accept. I couldn't have lost them all. Life couldn't be that cruel.

Maybe it wasn't. Maybe they were only injured and needed my help. Maybe I was wrong.

Those thoughts were exactly what I needed to face whatever was waiting inside for me. With determined steps, I got up and went to the door that had been left open, and my futile hope was dashed away just as quickly as it had arrived.

My eyes slammed shut and I braced myself in the doorway, but it was too late. I'd already seen too much.

Blood splattered along the living room walls, gore I couldn't identify covered the couch, and my baby brother's body was just mere feet from where I stood.

Fresh tears ran rivulets down my cheeks while I attempted to take steadying breaths. Teddy was so close to me. I just needed to find the strength to go to him like I had our mother. He deserved that.

Sliding to my knees, I opened my eyes and crawled the rest of the way to him. My vision was blurred, but even through the tears, there was no mistaking what I saw.

Bite marks marred his neck—at least the parts that hadn't been torn out with unnecessary force—and his body lay at an unnatural angle. Yet, there was no blood seeping from his wounds.

I averted my gaze from the awfulness, only to find remnants of my father's body scattered over the floor of the living room.

There was no saving them. They were already gone. My family was...dead. Just thinking the words caused pain in my chest like I'd never felt before.

I stayed on the floor next to my brother, convulsions rocking my body until a weariness began to stifle the agony of my losses. Sleep tried to claim me, my mind unable to process the hurt any longer, but the images of what I'd witnessed never faded from my thoughts.

I didn't know who those men had been, or why they'd chosen my family, but their faces were seared into my memory alongside the screams from my mother and the nightmare left inside the house.

The more I focused on those things, the less sadness filled me, but that didn't mean emotions weren't ravaging through me.

Rage took precedence as I considered what I needed to do next. I was only fourteen, but my mother had taught me how to survive—almost as if she'd known this day might come.

Her constant reminders of how strong and capable I was echoed through my mind as I finally sat up, turning to stare out the front door instead of further into the house.

Stars twinkled above and the moon shone brightly, but I'd find no solace within them tonight.

Surrounded by the remains of my family, I made a vow. I'd find the vile men who had done this. I'd figure out what they were and how I could make them pay for what they'd done.

As the declaration formed into something I could latch onto, I knew there was no going back to who I was before tonight.

I'd become whoever I needed to be, and do whatever it took, to claim the vengeance I sought.

No matter the cost.

1

Present day

RED WINE SWIRLED IN THE GLASS OF THE PATRON OPPOSITE me at the bar. I leaned back in the stool, grinning as the crimson color reminded me of blood. Something that used to make me cringe, but now I reveled in its darkness.

"Another whiskey, Amersyn?" Dave, the delicious yet untouchable—at least by me—bartender from Crossroads asked. He was well over six feet tall and had auburn hair that he kept short and spiked up at the top. His blue eyes were so light, they were almost silver.

"I think I'm going to call it a night. You good to close up by yourself?" Dave wasn't exactly my friend—I tried not to have those—but I wasn't heartless. Plus, I liked him. He was a human working in a supernatural bar. Someone needed to look out for the guy.

"Yeah, Steve is picking me up for a late-night-date-night." Dave waggled his brows, and I shook my head with a grin. Clearly, we were both having a good evening.

Crossroads was located in the shadiest part of Portland, Oregon, but it was my favorite place to go after winding down from a hunt. Plus, as a hunter, it was smart to know what my enemy was up to. I'd never been one to strike up a conversation with the vampires, shifters, and witches that frequented the bar, but it was easy to overhear things.

Sure, the supernaturals didn't like hunters hanging in the bar, but the gritty place was neutral territory for all of us. The owner and retired hunter Chester Dean only had two rules: no blood could be shed on his property and if you broke something, you replaced it. Glasses tended to go flying through the room every night, so it was a good rule for Chester's overhead.

I threw double the amount I needed to pay for my tab on the bar top and exited the building. Leaving Crossroads meant an attack could come at any moment, so while my posture was relaxed, my eyes saw everything, and my ears were attuned to the sounds of the city.

I had a witch to thank for my enhanced senses. When she found out that I wasn't some human groupie trying to get turned, she gifted me increased speed, healing, and smell. Nothing that made me anywhere near as strong as the bloodsuckers, but gave me more of a fighting chance, and thankfully, the increased smell only worked if I inhaled deeply. I wasn't sure I'd survive smelling death every time I hunted.

After the witch had cast her spell, she disappeared before I could figure out where she was from or get her full name. All she'd gone by to the other supernaturals within the bar was J. One day, maybe we'd cross paths again so I could properly thank her.

As I turned the corner outside—officially off Chester's property—a hand reached for me and I grabbed onto the accompanying wrist, twisting until the imbecile cried out.

"Damn, Amersyn. What's got a thong stuck up your ass crack?" Simon's nasally voice sounded, grating on my nerves. He was a hunter like me, so I tolerated him, but there was something about him I didn't trust. He reminded me of someone I used to know and that wasn't a good thing.

"First, that question makes absolutely no sense. Thongs are meant to go up people's asses—uncomfortably so. Second, haven't you learned by now? This *is* me in a good mood." I bent his arm a little further before shoving him away with a bright smile plastered to my face.

His mousy brown hair was matted, and his dull blue eyes roamed over me. I scrunched my nose at the smell coming from his wrinkled clothes, assuming he hadn't changed in days.

"I've been tracking a nest of ten. You want in?" Simon asked. Assumption confirmed.

Before he was finished with his sentence, I was

backing up. "I'm going to have to pass."

"Oh, come on. Derik was supposed to help me out, but he bailed last minute. I don't want to let these vamps pass by thinking they can come back anytime."

Simon had a point there, but I had rules—very specific ones that I lived by—and they'd never steered me wrong. Not since I learned how necessary they were.

The first rule was that I rarely worked with other hunters. It was rare to find someone who you could trust to have your back regardless of what they got out of it.

No matter the job, no matter the place, I trusted no one. A mistake I'd only made once when I first found out about hunters. I'd been naïve then. Years later, I was twenty-one, and maybe that was still young to some, but my mind was beyond that of normal humans my age after all I'd witnessed.

Simon tapped his foot and I sighed. "You know my—"

He cut me off. "Yeah, your rules. Blah, blah, blah. How do you ever expect to make waves if you don't join up with other hunters?"

I grunted. I had no desire to make waves. I just wanted to make a dent. A dent that included five particular vampires. Three had already been turned to ash. Two remained elusive, but I was motivated enough to never give up. I knew the reward of avenging my family was waiting for me, as long as I did everything right.

I wouldn't ever waver. I couldn't.

"Sorry, Simon. If you're not up for the task, give me the location and I'll take the job for you," I said, brushing my ebony hair out of my face as the icy wind blew around us.

Simon laughed, the stench of his cigarette breath wafting over me. "No can do. I'll find someone else to partner with. You have yourself a good night, Amersyn."

My skin crawled at the way he purred my name. I should have changed it long ago when I began hunting, but then I decided what I went by didn't matter. A name was nothing without the family that gave it to you.

I sighed, thinking of my parents and baby brother. Teddy hadn't actually been a baby—he'd only been ten months younger than me—but I'd taken my role as big sister very seriously.

Losing the three of them changed everything. Their deaths unleashed a darkness within me I'd never known possible. I should have been afraid of the rage and drive to kill, but instead, I'd reveled in the strength that the emotions provided me.

Vampires didn't deserve to walk our earth. They were nothing but parasites that people like me lived to extinguish.

When I learned they were real, I'd had more than

one misconception about them. First, the bastards bled, unlike I'd assumed before. While it wasn't their blood keeping them alive, the liquid still splattered when their heads were chopped off. Second, they could sleep like humans, but they didn't need to. Third, the bloodsuckers could eat normal food to blend in if needed.

So many things made them humanlike, but I'd been patient enough to figure out the quirks that also made them stand out.

After Simon scampered off, I headed back to my studio apartment above a local gym. I'd been living there for the last two years. I had a couple of safehouses —some much nicer than where I was staying—but I preferred to be closer to where the monsters liked to play. Comfort didn't come in the form of material things for me.

The owner Pete was a retired veteran who didn't ask questions, a good guy I didn't mind being around even during my worst moods. He held the same darkness in his eyes that I had in my own mahogany ones.

It also helped that Pete knew nothing about what I did during the night hours and never asked, either. As long as I didn't bring trouble to his doorstep, our arrangement worked out great with a don't-ask-don't-tell agreement.

When I arrived at the gym, the outside light to the back stairs was flickering, welcoming me home. I headed up the stairs that led to my room. I'd been back earlier after my latest kill—one that yielded me no new information—dropping off my crossbow and cleaning up before heading to Crossroads. Now, I was ready for sleep.

Entering my private space, I paused and inhaled. Something wasn't right.

My pillow was upside down from how I'd positioned it after making my bed that morning. The toothbrush on my bathroom sink had been moved, and my hair tie was missing. Shit. I knew I'd been staying here longer than any other place before, but I'd been more careful. Or at least, I thought I had been.

I tried not to panic. This wasn't the first time I'd had to bail without notice. I took a calming breath and another cursory glance through the room. Someone was messing with me, but I wasn't going to stick around long enough for them to come back and corner me.

Without wasting time, I went to my closet and grabbed my black duffle. It was time to leave. There was no postponing. That would only get me killed, and my purpose on this earth wasn't finished yet.

My important belongings were already packed, so all I had to do was throw whatever clothes I could fit inside and be on my way. I had duplicates of most things at my nearest safehouse. Anything else could be replaced.

Within sixty seconds, I was headed out the back exit. Anger was rising inside me at being forced out. I'd tried to keep it buried. Dwelling on emotions wasn't something I often did, not after my years of hunting, but this was personal and the longer I thought about that, the more I wasn't okay.

Every step away from the gym felt heavy. I knew I was making the right choice, but that didn't make me feel better about it, either.

A plan was already forming in my head. After getting my stuff from the apartment, I needed my crossbow from the alley, and then I'd head to the safehouse. It wasn't where I liked to stay on just any occasion—that defeated the purpose of it being a sanctuary when needed—but the condo would work until I sorted something else out. Worst case, I'd move north to Seattle a little earlier than planned.

Once I was outside, I took a moment to calm myself. This was the life I signed up for when my family died. There was no room for weakness. I had to be strong even when I didn't want to be. So many times, I'd thought to walk away and be done with the craziness of a world that shouldn't exist, but all I had to do was close my eyes.

The images of my parents and brother made my throat burn, and I was reminded of why I kept hunting these vampires, of why I couldn't ever give up.

After taking a moment to myself, I scanned the alley one last time. There wasn't anything out of the ordinary, so I quickly grabbed my crossbow from my hiding spot in the brick wall behind the dumpster. Tossing it over my head, the leather strap fit snugly across my chest, and I had everything I needed.

Taking a breath, I said a silent goodbye to the gym, then headed into the darkness of the night.

The safehouse was on the other side of Portland. A condo amongst the rich that paid no attention to the likes of me.

My car was already stashed there since I had nowhere to keep it at the gym—Portland streets weren't known for their plethora of parking spots—which meant I was best off heading back toward Crossroads. A few taxis were always waiting there for the drunks to take home, but most drivers rarely came back. I tried not to think too hard about why that was.

One block from my destination, the back of my neck tingled. My steps slowed as I listened for sounds behind me. There was nothing to be heard, but that didn't mean something wasn't there. I released my bag and turned around.

"I'm not in the mood for games tonight. Come on out." I left the bow on my back for the moment, counting on the knives I kept in the side pockets of my leather pants to be my first line of defense.

A soda can rolled across the darkened street. Someone was definitely there. I took a deep inhale, mentally preparing myself for the putrid smell of blood and decaying flesh to hit me.

Three vampires. Damn, that was more than I usually took on without being on the offense, but I had some extra aggressions to take out, so that would work in my favor.

"We just want to talk," a man's voice said from somewhere higher up.

I chuckled. "That's what they all say."

Movement was on my right, and I threw one of my knives into the shadows. Hissing sounded soon after, letting me know I'd hit my mark. Vampires were fast, and while I was quicker on my feet than a normal human, I still couldn't outrun a bloodsucker. Every move I made had to count.

"Now, that wasn't nice," another male voice sneered. The silver blade wouldn't kill a vampire unless I took their head off with it, but the metal would still burn like a mother.

I pulled my crossbow from my back and loaded a stake. As soon as one of the bastards stepped into my sights, they'd be dead from the poisonous tip.

My stakes were all custom-made from cedar, soaked in holy water, and stamped with a crucifix just below the silver tips mixed with dead man's blood. It was more than what was needed to make the stake, but one couldn't be too careful.

The first male I'd heard before spoke up again. "You killed our friend tonight, and several more last week. That's a problem we can't ignore any longer, Hunter."

"Yeah, I totally feel you there. I find it hard to ignore problems, too. You know, like when I catch one of you assholes sucking the life out of my kind."

One of the vampires was breathing harder than the others. My dagger must have hit better than I thought. I trained my ears to the sound of the panting and focused my crossbow in the same direction.

Without hesitation, I pulled the trigger and readied another stake, waiting for more vampires to attack.

A body thudded to the ground, but I couldn't pay him any mind as the other two came into view. Each of them had glowing red eyes, telling me they'd recently fed, which meant their strength would be up.

As if my night couldn't get any worse.

2

BEFORE EITHER OF THE BLOODSUCKERS MOVED, I PULLED the trigger on my crossbow and grinned as the vampire's eyes widened. Yeah, that asshole was going to be joining his friend in a matter of seconds. I had no time to watch his cold body shrivel up, though.

The nearest one disappeared and reappeared inches away from me, grabbing on to my neck and squeezing with his fangs elongated. I swallowed a gag while reaching for another blade. With one swift knee to his balls and a jab into his neck, the vampire released me, curling onto the ground.

I thought I was in good shape with two of the three already down before the fight had really even gotten started, but as I moved in to finish off the third, I heard more of them coming. Their hisses echoed off the brick walls within the alley.

I never could figure out why vampires thought

sounding like a pissed-off cat was intimidating. The sound was more like nails on a chalkboard to me.

Before the others showed their faces, I channeled my enhanced senses and readied for a fight until I realized the one I'd just stabbed was missing.

Fangs sliced down my arm as I started to roll out of the way. The vampire behind me had nearly ripped my neck out, but I could ignore the gouges on my bicep for the time being thanks to adrenaline and my accelerated healing.

Two more vampires appeared in the shadows, stalking closer to me. I only had three more stakes in my crossbow and two more daggers stashed in my boots. That should have been more than enough, but with them working together, I had a feeling kill shots wouldn't be as easy as I'd like.

The newcomers wasted no time taking their chance at claiming my life. Their bodies became a blur as they sped for me, and I did the same. I wasn't as fast as the vampires, but fast enough for enclosed areas like the alley.

One of them slammed his fist against the wall I'd been near, and the other circled back, diving toward me. We tumbled to the grimy ground, rolling with the force of his impact until we hit a stack of crates and I lost hold of my crossbow. *Damn it!*

The crate at the top crashed onto the ground next to us, breaking into pieces. I grabbed one of the shattered pieces of wood and stabbed it into the bloodsucker's neck. He wailed, releasing his hold on me, and I kicked him with as much force as I had in me.

I scrambled for my crossbow, but by the time my fingers wrapped around the stock, one of the vampires had a hold of my ankle. He picked me up like I was nothing until I was dangling in the air.

"Did you think you were going somewhere, Hunter?" he sneered.

"Nope. Just needed this." I didn't hesitate as I pulled the trigger, sending a stake into the asshole's junk.

He dropped me onto the ground, my head hitting the asphalt with an audible thud, and a wave of nausea came over me. Yeah, that was going to leave a mark.

I wiped my forehead and found more blood. That was not good. There were very few times that a vampire had made me bleed. Getting this close and personal with the vamps wasn't something I was fond of.

As I got up, I knew things weren't looking good for me, but there wasn't an ounce of give-up in my body. I still had two specific vampires to kill, and I wouldn't let these low-level bloodsuckers get in the way of the vow I made seven years ago.

Blood dripped down my face from my head wound, and I was having a hard time breathing, which meant I probably had fractured or broken ribs. Regardless, I took a step forward and brought my crossbow up.

"Who's next?" I asked with a twisted smile.

Before the vampires could decide what to do, we

had two more guests. My sights moved from the ones in front of me to the new arrivals behind them.

I wanted to scream in frustration. The vamps I'd only managed to injure were also beginning to stir, and I didn't know where the bigger threat lay—with those I was already fighting or the two remaining in the shadows.

Screw it. I acted without thinking too much. There was a decent possibility I was dying in this alley, and I at least wanted to turn as many of these assholes into ash as I could.

I shot one of the vampires in the back when he was distracted by the newcomers, hitting his heart. The other blurred and slammed into me, but I was prepared for that. I'd grabbed my second-to-last blade and jabbed the silver-coated metal into his neck as we landed on the ground, ten feet from where I'd been standing.

Damn, I was going to be covered in bruises after this fight. Thankfully, they wouldn't last long.

The vampire slammed his head into mine before rolling off me to rip the metal out of his neck. He wasn't as affected as the other had been, which meant he was older. I needed to aim only for his heart.

My crossbow was inches from my hand, but instead of grabbing the weapon, I took the next stake lined up between the risers and lifted the wooden object just in time for the vampire to land back on top of me.

His mouth formed into an O as the metal tip pierced his heart. The vamp's dead weight pressed down on me, sending the stake further into his chest. His skin began to suck in on itself as the rapid decomposition began its process. I pushed him off me, a task that required more effort than usual, and moved back just far enough to avoid the burst of ash that shimmered under the moonlight.

The newcomers had split up and one of them was ripping the head off the remaining bloodsucker I hadn't killed. Confusion pulsed through me, but I had no desire to stick around long enough to understand why they were killing their own kind.

I was still losing blood, not only from the head wound, but also the gouge on my arm from the fangs. Crossroads was only another hundred feet away. If I could get there and catch Dave before he left, I knew I could figure out my next move.

Footsteps moved toward me as I stayed crouched on the ground. I had one dagger left and no other stakes loaded into my crossbow.

The odds weren't great, but I still had fight left in me. These monsters wouldn't see me surrender.

When the vampire was standing over me, he reached down and grabbed under my shoulders. The gesture was gentle, but I wasn't buying that they'd helped me for any other reason than to get their own snack.

Using every ounce of energy I could muster, I pushed up from the ground and slammed a blade into the dark-skinned vampire's upper chest near his shoulder, not at all where I'd intended to hit him. Muddy red eyes widened at me in shock, and there was something about him that made me second-guess what I'd just done. He wasn't trying to fight back.

My head shook. No, that couldn't be right. Vampires didn't help anyone other than themselves. Vile effing creatures.

The second one hadn't moved, but I doubted whatever held him captive would last long. I got to my feet, grabbed my crossbow, and went for my bag. The other vamp was still staring at me. His eyes were the same dark red as the guy I'd stabbed. He wore black military-style clothes that were in pristine condition. Dark hair fell over his ears, and his square jaw was covered in a light layer of stubble. I couldn't tell if it was the start of a beard or laziness in shaving. Either way, it was working for him.

I mentally smacked some sense into myself. None of that mattered. He was a vampire. Attraction meant nothing. I had a window of opportunity I couldn't miss.

With my belongings in hand, I backed out of the alley. Well, more like hobbled. I was fueled only by adrenaline at that point.

When I got to the corner, I took one last peek to see if the two vampires were attempting to follow me. The tall, mysterious one had finally moved and was kneeling over his friend. He looked up and met my stare.

His eyes were hard and darkening, which shouldn't have been possible for a vampire. Not that I knew of anyway. The shock of whatever had gotten to him earlier was wearing off. I took that as my cue to get the hell out of there. I was in no condition to kill them.

I staggered my weary ass to Crossroads just in time to see Dave getting into his boyfriend's car. "Hey," I called out pathetically.

Dave turned, half inside the car already. "What the hell, Am?"

He came running toward me and took the bag I was barely managing to carry as my adrenaline waned. "Dirty bloodsuckers," I muttered.

Dave's boyfriend joined us. "And this is why I pick you up whenever possible," Steve muttered to Dave. He was just as good-looking as my bartender. Steve had blond hair and hazel eyes that held heaps of compassion within them. He always wore polo shirts with at least two buttons popped open. Tonight's was a black number I hoped I wouldn't be getting blood on.

They both loved the gym and fitness, so it was no hardship for Steve to wrap his arms around me and help me to his car while Dave tossed my bag into the trunk.

Once we were all settled into the vehicle, I looked out the window and didn't see either of the two vampires from the alley. They had confused the hell out of me. They'd had every chance to kill me. I'd been moving at a snail's pace when I left that alley and yet... they'd let me live. Something I'd have to think harder on after some rest.

"To the hospital where you *should* go, or somewhere else?" Dave asked. Nobody I knew was aware of where

I lived. I made a point to keep that as secret as I could so the fact that I didn't point Steve in the direction of the gym wasn't a red flag.

"Is it too far out of the way to head toward Ross Island Bridge?" I asked. There was a park only a few blocks from my condo near there. I'd walk the rest of the way and hope nobody called the cops on my torn-up ass.

Steve winked at me. "Nothing is too far for the woman who helps keep my man safe."

I narrowed my eyes at Dave. He wasn't supposed to share what he knew about the patrons of Crossroads with anyone—a condition I knew was part of his employment with Chester. Dave merely shrugged. He was lucky I liked him.

Steve drove away from the bar. He was headed in the direction that would take us right past the alley where I'd been attacked. My gaze focused on the darkened street, but there was nothing left to see. The dead vampires had all become nothing more than ash taken away by the wind, and the two others were nowhere to be seen.

I shoved the worry that they were following us aside and closed my eyes. I hadn't been this banged up in a while. My head had finally stopped bleeding, but my arm was throbbing. I glanced down to find black ooze crusting around the scrapes from the vampire's teeth. The bastard had gotten venom into my system, but without forcing his tainted blood down my throat, the venom was nothing more than an annoyance. And it explained why I'd tired out faster than usual.

Before I knew it, Dave was gently shaking me awake. "We're at the park. Where to next?"

I sat up with a groan. "Here is good. A friend is picking me up."

He raised a pointed brow. "I thought Amersyn Holt didn't have friends?"

I said nothing in return. I didn't have the energy to keep making up lies. Instead, I got out of the car and headed to the trunk. It popped open, and I waved my thanks to Steve who was still in the driver's seat. Dave followed me and was suddenly shirtless.

Sculpted and tan muscles reflected under the moon's light. "Take this." He handed me his long-sleeved Henley.

"Uhh, why?" I asked.

"Because you look like a serial killer."

Well, he wasn't wrong about that.

I set my crossbow down and put the grey shirt on. The hem fell to my mid-thigh, and the sleeves covered the injury on my arm.

Dave reached into the trunk next, pulling out a ball cap. "Take this, too. And don't worry about returning any of it."

"Thanks, Dave." I said the words as sincerely as I could while I folded the front of my crossbow in on itself and shoved the weapon into my bag.

"I'm happy to help. You know I won't push you for

more than you're willing to share, but I hope you know I'm here for you anytime, Amersyn," he said sincerely.

"I know and I appreciate that even if I'm bad at showing it," I said with a grimace.

"I'll see you soon." Dave smiled at me before getting back into the passenger seat.

What I loved about the bartender was that I knew I could believe his words. Dave was always willing to help or be there to complain to about shitty nights, but he never pried. He understood my need for privacy and wasn't offended by my lack of trust. It was just part of a hunter's life.

After their taillights disappeared, I opened my bag and fished out the card that would allow me entrance into my condo. The building had million-dollar views of Portland and came with the same figure price tag.

With the money I'd inherited from my parents, I splurged on real estate in the Pacific Northwest where the highest population of vampires were. Some of the places I invested in were worse than slumlord rentals and others not so much. This condo was a treat after I killed the first vampire responsible for the deaths of my family. I had zero regrets.

It took twice as long as it should have to get to the building made mostly of glass and steel, and once I did, I nearly cried tears of joy, but then the doorman tried to stop me.

"You're in the wrong part of Portland, miss. We don't want any trouble from your kind," he said, looking down on me like I was some homeless chick trying to rob them.

I sneered and showed him my access card. "Move."

He stuttered, addressing me by one of my many aliases. "Oh, Ms. Smith. I'm sorry. We haven't seen you in some time, and I—"

"And I don't care. Move. Now."

My patience had run out, and I was taking it out on the poor guy. I'd apologize tomorrow or the next day. Whenever I surfaced again.

The doorman moved out of my way, and I continued toward the elevators. I pressed my bloodied finger against the metal button, uncaring when some of my dried blood smeared against it.

A ding sounded just as the doors opened. I tossed my bag inside before lifting my card to the screen. I had to adjust it twice before the stupid scanner accepted it.

"Welcome home, Ms. Smith," an automated voice sounded in the elevator as the doors closed.

Yeah, home. That was a subjective word.

3

MY BED WAS MADE IN HEAVEN. I WAS CERTAIN OF IT. SLEEP was never better than when I crashed in this condo. I should have bought another safehouse and made this one my regular home, but it wasn't conveniently located to where I hunted most, and that was an issue.

The hunter struggle was real.

When I woke up, I had no idea what time it was, thanks to my blackout shades and lack of clock in my room, but as awareness came back to me, an uneasiness took over.

I wasn't alone.

It was a good thing I never slept unarmed. My hand reached for the stake I kept under my pillow, but it wasn't there.

"Looking for this?" a masculine, yet sultry voice said.

I turned over slowly. The guy I unfortunately hadn't shot back in the alley was sitting in a chair next to my bed, twirling said stake between his fingers. Shit, this wasn't good. Especially since I was naked as the day I was born.

With my sage green silk sheet tucked around me, I reached for my bedside lamp. The finer details of the vampire came into view, and I nearly gasped. He wasn't at all the same as the night before.

He was dressed in a black suit with a crisp white shirt beneath it, but no tie. No, he was too suave for that accessory. Instead, he kept the top three buttons undone, showing off a light smattering of chest hair.

His coffee-colored hair was parted down the middle, and he pushed a loose piece behind his ear as his muddy-red eyes appraised me. His eye color was the exact same as his friend's that I'd stabbed, though I swore they'd been darker as I walked away from the alley. Questions about why that might be ran through my mind briefly until I realized that detail didn't matter.

What was most important was why and how this bloodsucker was in my condo.

"What do you want?" I asked.

"Well, you tried to kill my friend when all we'd done was help you. Maybe I've come to repay the favor," he said calmly.

"If that was the case, I'd already be dead. Unless you prefer to play with your food like a psycho." I eyed him openly, then added, "Wouldn't be surprised."

He scoffed at my insult. "I don't play. I take what I want."

Yeah, he was as much of a prick as his suit made him appear.

"So, like I asked before, what do you want?" I asked.

He held the stake with his left hand and his right pointer finger hovered over the tip. "Why do you use so many extra ingredients in your weapon?"

I barked out a laugh. "You want to know about my weapons?"

"More of a curiosity. You're different from most hunters I've encountered before."

Damn right, I was. I was more careful, but I wasn't going to tell this arrogant jerk that.

"I'm different for a reason." And I was also over sitting in my bed as if he had the upper hand on me. I rolled off the mattress, leaving my sheet behind, and taking the risk that this vampire wasn't in a hurry to fight me.

With one glance back, I caught him smirking and nodding at me. "Yes, I'd have to agree."

I entered my walk-in closet without replying and wiggled into fresh underwear and jeans before peeking my head back out into the room. The vamp hadn't moved, but he was watching me and still clutching my stake. I didn't take him for an idiot and, sure enough, when I reached into the back of my underwear drawer, the stake that should have been there was gone. Stupid, smart prick.

Grabbing a bra and shirt, I slipped those on before opening the other drawers in search of a weapon.

"Sixteen of them, Amersyn. That's how many stakes

I found in your room," he called, still sitting relaxed in my chair.

"Listen here, mother—" I came storming out of my closet, finger pointed in his direction, but he was gone within the blink of an eye. Until he wasn't.

His breath was suddenly on my neck. "No, you listen, and I talk."

Holy hell. My stomach clenched, and everything within me wanted to lean back into him. Damn, there was something seriously wrong with me. I must have hit my head harder than I realized in that alley.

Steeling my resolve, I took a step forward before turning around to face him. "If you didn't notice, this is my house. You don't get to make the rules here."

"Given that your house is located within the territory I run, I think I do."

I stared at his face. He'd shaved before coming to find me. His skin was like rock, a smooth and perfectly sculpted one.

I shook my head. *Get your crap together, Amersyn.*

"So, you're a nest leader for South Portland. What were you doing on the east side last night?" I asked.

He shook his finger at me, closing the distance I'd just created. "No, Amersyn. I'm asking the questions."

Our chests were nearly touching, my skin warming and stomach tightening, but I didn't back away this time. He didn't need to know he was affecting me. "How do you know my name?"

"I've learned a lot about you lately, especially in the last fourteen hours. Unfortunately, there is still a lot that doesn't make sense." A line formed between his two symmetrical eyebrows.

That was the first time he'd shown a weakness. He didn't have all of the information he wanted, and that frustrated him. Good. Bastard deserved that for breaking into my house.

"What about me doesn't make sense?" I asked before turning away from him to head into the kitchen. If I was going to survive a civil conversation with a vampire before I killed him, I needed coffee.

Opening my bedroom door, I peeked out the front windows to find the sun was already setting for the day. The oranges and purples mixed together, almost distracting me from the caffeine I badly needed.

"I also found the nine other stakes in your kitchen, so don't bother," the vampire droned.

Again…stupid, smart prick.

"What's your name so I can maybe stop calling you 'prick' in my head?" I asked as I opened the pantry to grab my coffee.

He chuckled. "Maciah West."

"Sounds like a prick kind of name. Fitting."

He was next to me before I drew another breath. The vampire inhaled deeply at my neck, causing my insides to twist in ways I was trying to pretend weren't happening. Under no circumstances would I be attracted to a vampire. It couldn't be possible.

"You're not afraid of me," Maciah said.

"Why should I be? You're either going to kill me, or

I'm going to kill you. Whatever happens next is up to fate."

I took a step away from him and went to my coffee maker, double checking the drawer beneath it for a stake. I had no idea how many stakes I had lying around. I just knew there were a lot of them. Even though Maciah had found nine, that didn't mean anything to me. Plus, looking for them gave me something else to focus on.

Unfortunately, that one was gone, so I grabbed three packets of sugar instead. I scooped out the delicious granules of coffee, poured them carefully into my tiny refillable cup, and popped it into the coffee maker.

Closing the lid, I double-checked there was enough water and pressed the strong button to get my coffee as potent as possible. I had a feeling I was going to need the extra boost.

Maciah moved to the other side of my counter, sitting on one of the stools while I leaned against the stainless-steel refrigerator.

"You don't live here often," Maciah said as if he knew me, then added, "Your scent isn't strong in most parts of the condo."

"How about you quit procrastinating and say what you need to? Obviously, you're a patient person, but I am not. I have things I need to do today that don't include making small talk with a bloodsucker."

He sneered at my choice of words, but I didn't care. He was what he was, and I needed to keep that at the forefront of my mind.

"Do you know why your wounds have already begun healing?" he asked, surprising me with the change of direction.

"Because I take good care of my body and it does the same in return," I answered. He didn't need to know that a witch assisted me with enhanced traits that helped level the playing field between me and the vampires I hunted.

I knew that if I removed the bandages on my forehead and bicep, the wounds from the night before would be closing already. And my bruises? I didn't need to look in the mirror to know they'd gone from purple to green. By tomorrow, they'd be yellowing.

My ribs, on the other hand, were still affecting me and would be for at least a few days. Though, I was well aware that was something that should have taken weeks to heal for any normal human.

Maciah narrowed his burnt-red eyes on me. "Do you really believe that?"

"Why wouldn't I?" Maybe he knew about my enhancements and didn't believe me. Either way, I knew who I was and didn't care if he agreed with my reasoning.

"Okay. Tell me about your parents?" he asked, and I sucked in a breath. A vice tightened around my heart. I didn't talk about my parents with anyone. Not ever. Nobody even knew I had a brother before. Not anyone who knew me anymore.

"That's none of your damn business," I answered, turning back for my coffee. My cup still had room in it, so I reached up to grab the whiskey. I was going to need a double boost to deal with this vampire.

"Actually, I believe it is. Tell me who they were," Maciah demanded.

I considered tossing my scalding hot drink in his face but decided not to waste the deliciousness. Instead, I turned slowly around with a smile on my face.

"You can kindly get the hell out of my house now. You might have stolen all of my stakes, but that doesn't mean I can't hurt you if you choose to continue pissing me off," I said with feigned sweetness.

"Like you hurt Zeke? Do you pride yourself on being a murderer? I bet that makes mommy and daddy very proud," he countered.

Screw this prick.

I threw my drink at his face, but he was already gone from the stool. I swung my arm back, sensing him behind me, and my fist cracked against his jaw. He grabbed my ribs, and I nearly passed out from the pain before reaching for the knife block. I was about to cut this asshole, even if it wouldn't kill him.

My fingers grazed the handles before Maciah blurred with me still in his arms. I was suddenly pressed against the cool glass of my floor-to-ceiling windows, facing Maciah's scowling lips.

He let out a small hiss, pressing closer to keep my arms trapped. "Quit trying to kill me."

"If you'd have left when I told you to, I wouldn't be." I tilted my chin, meeting his piercing eyes. He was different. I couldn't deny that like I was the attraction simmering inside me.

Maciah might not be the usual vampire I hunted, but he still had to drink human blood to survive, and that was all that mattered to me—that was all it took to make him enemy number one in my book.

"Do you really have no clue?" he asked, eyes pinched as he appraised me.

"About what?" I snapped.

Maciah's hands tightened painfully around my biceps. Our bodies were still flush against each other, and the only thing that kept me from melting into a puddle from the growing heat between us was the iciness of the window behind me.

He stared me down, waiting for some sort of sign. Finally, he sighed, loosening his hold ever so slightly.

"You're a vampire, Amersyn."

4

I LAUGHED SO HARD THAT MY SPIT LANDED ON MACIAH'S face. Sure, he was different from most vampires I met, but he was also beyond insane. He thought *I* was a vampire? Freaking hilarious.

"You're out of your damn mind. I am the furthest thing from a vampire there is," I said once the hysterics within me settled.

Maciah's eyes flashed a crimson, the brown in them fading to the background. "Did you just spit on me?"

I shrugged, moving further away from him. Gone was the calm, business-like vampire, and in his place was the monster I assumed him to be. My cedar table was between us, and I knew I should have had two more stakes under the tabletop. If he hadn't found those, I might be able to end the craziness of this conversation.

I put my hands on the smooth surface and leaned forward. "That's what happens when you say psychotic

41

things. People tend to laugh in your face," I said, trying to add fuel to the fire and distract him.

His eyes stayed on mine as I slowly moved one of my hands under the table. My fingers felt the metal tip of the stake, and I nearly sagged in relief. I was going to kill this vampire for breaking into my house and saying stupid things.

"I'm not lying to you, Amersyn. If you'd think for a minute, then you'd realize that. You're faster, stronger, and more resilient than any other human I've ever seen. That's not normal," he said.

I rolled my eyes, sneaking the stake behind my back as I replied. "I know that. A witch did some magic—"

He snarled and his fist slammed down on my table, putting a noticeable crack in the top. He was going to pay for that, too.

"No, a witch concealed your true identity. How can you be so naïve?" He was practically screaming by then, and I used his emotions to make my move.

"There is nothing naïve about me. I know exactly who I am and what my purpose is," I said as I leaped over the table, stake held tightly in my right hand, and aimed for his heart.

He blurred out of the way before I could hit my mark. He was fast, but I was persistent. He wasn't walking out of my condo.

Maciah bounced on the balls of both his feet, making it hard for me to guess which way he was going to move once I lunged for him again. I needed to be patient and learn his tells before I could end him.

I feigned to the left before striking right. He anticipated my move, shoving me to the ground, but I kept a tight hold of the stake. He'd have to pry the wood from my dead hands if he thought to take it from me.

"This is a waste of our time," he deadpanned as if I was no threat to him.

"Screw you," I spat, getting up to my feet.

"I'll have to pass on the offer this time," he taunted.

Arrogant. Prick.

I darted for him again. My ribs protested against the quick movements, but I ignored the pain, knowing the reward would be worth the extra few days of healing.

When I was close enough, I swung my stake, this time aiming for his leg instead of his heart. If I could injure him, he'd slow down enough for me to kill him easier.

The metal tip caught on his black slacks, tearing the dress pants, but missing the skin.

He frowned. "I liked these pants."

And I liked his ass in them, but I didn't really care about that. Vampires were all hot. That was part of their appeal to draw helpless humans in. Sure, Maciah was a notch above hot, but that didn't mean shit to me. He needed to die.

I jumped toward the table, intending to use the wooden surface to push off from, allowing me to go further than normal. Just as my toes touched the surface, Maciah's arms wrapped around my waist causing half my body to hang over his back.

Stupid, stupid, vampire.

I was upside down as his grip tightened around my thighs. With my stake ready, I aimed for his heart. There were no rules stating I couldn't stab him in the back, and I planned to do just that. As my weapon headed toward its target, he decided to roll us, causing the metal tip to cut through his rib and straight into my thigh.

Mother effer, that hurt!

"Burns, doesn't it?" Maciah said before throwing me onto the loveseat across the room.

Of *course* it burned. I'd stabbed myself. Wounds tended to do that.

I glanced down—it was only a surface scratch. My jeans had taken the brunt of the damage, thankfully.

Maciah stalked toward me as I got back up. His previously parted and brushed hair was disheveled, and he dropped his ruined suit coat to the floor before peeking at the blood dripping from his ribs. As he adjusted his shirt, I could see the puncture mark was already closing. He healed faster than most vampires. Not good for me. I had to get a kill shot in.

"I'd like to make you an offer," he said casually, even though his eyes were pulsing with irritation.

"I don't negotiate with blood terrorists," I retorted sharply.

He pinched the bridge of his perfectly straight nose and sighed. "Amersyn, you need to listen to me."

"Why would I ever do that?" I was up from the

couch, ready to continue our fight, but his next words made me pause.

"Because I know who you are."

I scoffed. "You don't know the first thing about me."

Nobody knew me. It was how I separated myself from the others and focused on what needed to be done. I couldn't care about other people. I couldn't let them in. They'd be something else I needed to fight for, and I wasn't sure I was capable of that. Not until I'd avenged my family.

"You were born twenty-one years ago. Your mother was Sondra McClaren. Your pseudo-father was Greg Holt. Your parents were killed seven years ago, along with a brother only ten months younger than you. I know five vampires were present that night. I know you've killed three and are in search of the other two, but you kill any vampire in your quest for vengeance and information." He paused, taking a deep inhale. "I know the blood of an original vampire runs through your veins."

The longer he spoke, the more rage I built up. How dare he speak of my family. How dare he pretend to know me just because he had a few facts that very people knew. I tried to keep my emotions out of my actions, because those only got people killed, but Maciah had broken through my walls, and I lost control.

With a guttural roar, I charged for him, and he merely stood there. I knocked him to the ground, stake still in hand. I raised the wooden weapon into the air, ready to end him. When he didn't fight back like before, I paused for the briefest of seconds, long enough for him to reverse our roles.

Maciah sat on top of me, my arms pinned underneath his strong, muscled legs. "I'm telling you the truth, Amersyn. I don't lie."

"Ha! Vampires are the creators of deceit." I bucked beneath him, knocking him forward so I could get my arm loose. I plunged the stake into his ribs, hoping to hit his heart from the side.

He grabbed both of my arms, pinned them above my head, and leaned over me. "Stop trying to kill me, damn it," he spat before reaching up to pull the stake from his side.

I took the opportunity to try to yank my hands free from his single-handed hold, but he only gripped me tighter. I started to wiggle beneath him, moving every way I could and hoping to throw him off me. Only I'd managed nothing of the sort.

Maciah used one hand to snap my only weapon in half before he pressed all of his weight onto me. His thighs were cool against my sides, making my skin feel as if it was simmering. He leaned in closer, strands of his dark hair falling forward as his crimson eyes faded back to muddy-red.

Once again, he inhaled deeply, sighing. A sound that seemed to be made from equal parts frustration, attraction, and curiosity.

"I'm not going to hurt you, Amersyn. I can't. But I

do need you to listen to me. You are as I've said. You can choose to believe it or not. That doesn't really matter to me. I do, however, need you to stop trying to kill me so I can offer you a deal you won't want to miss."

His tone was solemn, and my gut twisted at the thought that maybe it wouldn't be so bad to hear him out, even if he was delusional about some of his facts.

Then, I thought about what that said about me. Working with the same kind of monsters that killed my family? That would be the ultimate betrayal, yet a part of me was holding back. I could have ended Maciah already, but I'd paused for reasons I wasn't ready to explore yet.

Maciah must have seen something in my eyes, because he released my hands. I pushed against his chest until he was no longer on top of me. I needed some major space from him in order to think.

He had a deal to offer me. He knew why I hunted vampires. He knew more about me than anyone else, and he also believed something that couldn't possibly be true.

I was not a vampire.

I didn't crave blood. I didn't murder innocent humans. I didn't have venom tainting my veins.

As I stalked back toward the kitchen, I made myself a new cup of coffee. Maciah followed me, once again sitting at the counter and waiting for me to speak. I kept my back to him—a move I probably shouldn't have made considering I'd almost just killed him, but I didn't need him trying to read my face as I considered what I was going to do next.

I frequented Crossroads because it allowed me to get to know my enemy better. I was capable of being in the same room as those I hunted and not killing them, all in the name of information.

Maybe I could do the same with Maciah. Maybe I could convince him that I believed his bullshit and see what value he brought to the table. If this vampire could bring me closer to the monsters that killed my family, it would be worth whatever he wanted in return.

Before I got to that, I needed to know more about him. He had more control than any other vampire I'd interacted with, and his eyes changed colors. That wasn't normal.

With my new mug of whiskey-enhanced coffee, I finally turned back to the vampire. "Why do your eyes keep changing color?"

He shook his head. "That's the most important question right now?" I shrugged and he continued, "I learned early on how to gain control over my emotions, something very few vampires can do until they've lived a century or two. My eyes react to my feelings, darkening when I'm not exactly happy."

That was something to remember. "How old are you?" I asked next.

"Seventy-eight. I was turned when I was twenty-six. I have killed humans, but not in thirty years. Would you like to know my favorite color next?" he asked with a smirk.

I could be done with the personal questions, but only for the time being. I got back to our previous conversation. "What is your offer?"

"Do you believe what I've said?" he asked, suspicion filling his eyes.

"I don't think you're lying to me," I answered truthfully. Vampires could sense lies a mile away. I had to choose my words carefully.

"So, you believe you're a vampire?" he pressed.

Damn. He saw through my answer. I believed he thought he was telling the truth. There was no possibility of him being right, though.

I had my father's eyes and nose. Everything about us was similar except my hair color. He most certainly was not a vampire, and neither was my mother.

"I think there are a lot of things to consider before I can truthfully answer that. Isn't it enough that I stopped trying to kill you?" I asked.

He raised a brow. "For now, you've stopped."

The bloodsucker wasn't wrong about that.

"Are you going to tell me about this offer I don't want to miss out on, or not? I don't have time for any more games. Why were you and your friend in the alley last night, and why are you here now?" I took a long pull of my coffee, enjoying the burn from not only the temperature, but the whiskey as it slid down my throat. Maciah watched me with more curiosity as I kept the cup in front of my lips.

"I know of the group that was at your house seven years ago. Viktor, Rigo, Caesar, Igor, and Dmitri. You've killed all but Rigo and Dmitri. I can help you find them if you agree to kill one vampire for me before I do."

I nearly threw my coffee at him again. "Do you think I'm an idiot? Why would I do you a favor before getting anything in return? I don't need you. I can find these two on my own."

He smirked, only one side of his perfect lips lifting as his eyes sparked with life. I sucked in a breath. Crap, he was sexy as sin. Too bad he was a filthy bloodsucker. No matter how hot Maciah was, I wouldn't allow that to affect my decisions.

"Did you know Rigo and Dmitri are brothers from a Russian nest? One with a leader more ruthless than anything your *human* mind could fathom?"

He'd said human as a dig at my lack of belief, but I ignored that bit. "And your point is?"

"Unless you draw them out for a job, you're never going to get near them. These vampires aren't the street slum you're used to killing, Amersyn. They will end you first if you continue to work alone."

"I killed the first three just fine," I said before taking another drink from my mug.

Maciah snorted, something I didn't expect from the put-together vampire. "Those were throw-out vampires, ones used as a distraction for the main event to make their play. Rigo and Dmitri had no relation to them. That's why your trail has gone cold ever since killing Igor."

I didn't want to admit he was right. I hadn't learned anything new in months.

"Work with me, Amersyn, and I will get you your vengeance," Maciah said with conviction.

My first thought was to dismiss him. I had my rules that kept me safe, but I also relied on my instincts to guide me. A wave of warmth settled over me at the thought of working with this vampire. Something foreign, but not unappealing.

Could I really do this? Could I trust a vampire?

5

MACIAH LEFT SOON AFTER DROPPING THE BOMB THAT Dmitri and Rigo would be harder to find than I hoped. I sat on the loveseat long after I bolted my door shut, wondering what the hell had just happened. With his departure, my mixed emotions continued to wage a war inside me, leaving my mind even more confused.

A vampire had broken into my safehouse. I had no idea how he'd found me. I'd been certain nobody had been following me, but with the vampire bite, maybe my senses hadn't been working as well as I'd thought.

Then, the audacity of him to claim I was a monster just like him...I honestly couldn't believe it. I was normal before that witch came along. I had no supernatural skills. Anything I was before came by hard work and perseverance. The prick didn't know what he was talking about.

My father and mother were my only parents. I wasn't something other than what I'd known my whole life. I was human. I was a fighter. I was a vampire hunter.

I couldn't stop considering his offer, though. I didn't see how it could be a bad decision. I could placate the vampire, pretend I thought he was blabbering the truth. I'd get to kill another vampire—never a bad thing—and I'd get to avenge my family.

But could I work alongside Maciah without killing him before I got what I wanted?

Worse, could I work with him and not cross lines I'd never thought were an option before?

I wasn't stupid. Maciah was sexy, and he'd shown a kindness I'd never expect from a bloodsucker. There was an attraction between us, and it wasn't just one-sided. I'd seen the way he'd looked at me when I rolled out of my bed without any clothes.

I shook my head before I got too distracted and got up from the couch, then made my way to the balcony. Evening had fallen. I'd slept long enough to miss a whole day. I was still sore from the night before and from trying to kill Maciah, but I wasn't incapable.

Getting out of the house was a good thing. I needed to go to Crossroads and see if there was any word about the vampires from the night before. If one died, the others didn't normally come looking for vengeance. No, they moved on and created another bloodsucker to replace the last.

Why had they come for me?

As I leaned over the railing, taking in the sights of Portland, I knew I needed to figure out why before I went hunting again. I enjoyed working alone. Depending on just myself was the only way to ensure my safety.

Unless the vampires had grown tired of me killing them off and were working together. Or maybe Dmitri and Rigo figured out I was after them and they'd begun sending assholes after me.

I didn't know, and I wasn't going to find out by sitting at home.

WITHIN THE HOUR, I'D SHOWERED AND TAKEN MY TIME blow-drying my long ebony hair. As I stared in the mirror, I took in my pale skin and mahogany eyes, wondering if the signs had been there all along. Could it be possible Maciah was right? Was I a vampire and had no idea?

I rubbed a hand over my arm, inspecting the mark left behind from the vampire and thankful he hadn't ruined the tattoo on my opposite arm.

The tribal marks were a reminder of the promise I'd made the day my family died. The black lines spoke of strength and vengeance, something I could never forget. I was a hunter, not a vampire.

My emotions were at war, and I needed to get my thoughts back in order. Exiting the bathroom, I shook off any possibility that Maciah could be right. There was no way, and I needed to stick with that thought instead of continuing to waver. The witch had given me all of my enhanced abilities. That was the more logical explanation.

I went to the kitchen to grab a Hot Pocket for a quick dinner. Yes, they were disgusting, but they did the job of filling my stomach when I was in a hurry. When I opened the freezer door, I found all of my stakes, covered in frost. Freaking vampires.

Oddly enough, my crossbow was still near the door where I'd dropped it after barely making it inside my condo the night before. Maciah had only taken the items that could kill him, and he hadn't willingly laid a hand on me.

I still didn't understand that. Maybe a few shots of whiskey would clear things up for me.

After I ate my super healthy dinner, I drove to Crossroads in my black unmarked sports car. The two-door, hardtop Lexus was blacked-out, and unless someone was a real car enthusiast, most people never could figure out what I drove. I liked it that way.

As I parked in front of the bar, I patted the dashboard. "I won't be long, and if anyone touches you, I'll kill them."

Crossroads wasn't somewhere I trusted leaving my favorite car, but I had no other choice. I needed answers and a stiff drink served by my favorite bartender.

Walking in, the volume of voices was louder than normal. The usuals were all around, the sound of classic rock echoed around the room, and the scent of spilled alcohol wafted toward the door.

Dave was at the counter, serving a wolf shifter I'd

seen around, and the other bartender Toby was in as well. I sat down, and he came right over.

He smiled bright, revealing perfect teeth and dimples as he ran a hand over his buzzed blond hair. Toby wore a tight black shirt with the Crossroads logo in the middle and ripped, light-blue jeans.

"How's it going, Amersyn?" he asked with a nod.

"It's going. No offense, but I'm going to wait for Dave. I need to chat with him," I said, offering him a smile to lessen my rejection.

Toby gripped his chest dramatically. "Oh, how you wound me! Am I not even worthy to get you a double shot of Blanton's while you wait for him to finish with Harry?"

I laughed at the flirtatious bartender. "Toby, I would love a double shot, just from you."

He winked at me and bowed. "It would be an honor to serve you, My Lady."

Toby turned back to the bar, and Dave nodded at me while he was talking. I didn't miss how his eyes appraised me, checking for injuries.

"Here you are, gorgeous," Toby said as he slid me the whiskey glass.

I offered him a smile as he moved on to the next patron. While I waited for Dave, I focused my hearing on the tables around me, searching for any sort of information that might be useful.

Murmurs of parties, turf battles, new hook-ups, and the usual crap I didn't normally care about were all I could pick up, which disappointed me more than I cared to admit. Maciah had made me feel off-kilter—uncertain, even. I didn't like it one bit.

With that thought, I knew I had my answer. I couldn't trust the vampire. There would be no working with someone who acted superior to me, who thought they had leverage against me. No, I hadn't second-guessed my choices in a long time. I wouldn't go backwards. Not again.

I glanced back to see Dave waylaid by another customer. Damn, I could be here for a while.

My knee bounced along to the music while I continued to listen for anything worthwhile. I knew what I needed to do, and that made things easier. Once the decision was made not to work with Maciah, tension lifted from my shoulders, and I was ready for whatever the night would bring.

As I took a couple of pulls from my double shot, the door swung open so hard, its thud echoed through the room, causing more than half of us to turn and look.

A stunning female stood in the doorframe, fingers covering her mouth. "Oops," she said before taking a step inside and closing the door behind her.

I'd never seen this woman before, and because of the red tint to her eyes, I was curious about her arrival and what I might overhear from the vampire. She had long brunette hair with golden highlights and a swoop of bangs over the right side of her pale face.

She wore a one-piece black leather suit, knee-high stiletto boots, and a silver belt around her waist that I assumed was made from platinum—the only silver metal that didn't burn vampires.

I moved my gaze away from her once the other supernaturals and hunters in the bar did the same. I took another drink of my whiskey and checked on Dave again. He was glaring at the woman who'd slammed his door—a pet peeve of his that most people only did once. Dave could be scary when he wanted, like right then.

He sauntered toward me, eyes narrowed and lips thinned. The newcomer took a seat next to me, even though there were four other stools empty down the way. Definitely not what I was hoping for.

She waved at Dave, seemingly oblivious to the fact that she'd already irritated him. "Hey there, sex on a stick. Can you get me a Bloody Mary, extra blood, pretty please?" She fluttered her eyes, and he softened toward her.

"Don't ever slam that door again," he muttered before turning around. So much for scary Dave. I was hoping for some entertainment.

The vampire turned toward me, drumming her nails on the counter. I could feel her stare, but I had nothing to say, so I ignored her. That was until she kicked my boot.

"Hunter, I'd like to chat with you," she said.

"Kindly go piss off," I replied. I'd had enough of "talking" with vampires for the day. I had only been curious about what had brought her into the bar. If she was only there to chat with me, my interest was lost.

She continued to tap her fingers on the bar top, and I could see her lips pinched as if she was thinking extra hard.

Dave set her drink on the counter, then dropped the celery stick in. "You're new here," he said.

"New to this bar, yes. New to the area, absolutely not."

That, I found mildly intriguing.

"Well, we have a few rules around here," Dave began, but she waved him off with a soft giggle.

"I'm well aware, barkeep. I don't mind rules, and I intend to follow them, so long as everyone else does."

Dave nodded, then turned to me. "You good to wait a little longer? Busy night."

I nodded. "I can see that."

Dave moved to keep working, and I considered leaving to avoid my new company.

"So, are you really not interested in what I'd like to chat about?" the vamp asked.

I turned toward her slowly. "Unless you have a vampire that needs killing, then no, I don't care one bit."

She grinned, showing off pointed incisors. "I do, actually. You see, my friend tried to recruit you earlier for the job, but I've been told he doesn't believe you'll accept and that just won't do."

Maciah. Oh, how I wish I could have killed him in my condo.

"And why is that?" I asked.

"Because Maciah is my friend and he needs you to

do him a solid, which means I need you to do so as well."

I snorted. "If that prick is your friend, then why don't *you* kill the vampire in question?"

Her eyes flashed a deep crimson, and she lowered her head. "Oh, believe me. I'd love to. Extenuating circumstances prevent that from happening, though."

"Which would be what?" Maciah was a capable vampire. A nest leader, from the sounds of it. He was also old and powerful and...I didn't need to think of anything else. There shouldn't have been any reason why he couldn't handle his own business.

"Listen, Amersyn. That's not the point. I'm here because Maciah can be a real asshole sometimes, and when he mentioned trying to recruit you for this job, I was excited. There's not a lot to be excited about in our world, you know?"

Was this bloodsucker trying to get me to sympathize with her? Not effing happening.

"I know you hate vampires, but haven't you ever thought beyond that rage? Don't you realize that there are some of us out there that didn't choose this life? That just want to do the best they can with the shit sandwich they've been handed for dinner?"

She was pleading with me. Genuinely trying to get me to see her as something other than a monster. What was happening with my life? First, Maciah telling me I was a vampire, then this chick and her plea? No, I couldn't do it. I was a vampire hunter. I didn't work with the monsters I wanted to extinguish from the earth.

"Listen…whatever your name is."

"Rachel. The name is Rachel," she cut in.

I groaned. Such a normal name. Of course, it was. "Right. Rachel. I'm not one of you."

"Maciah said you'd say that." She grinned.

My fists tightened on the counter. "Don't interrupt me."

She pretended to zip her mouth and throw away the key like she was five. Seriously, I didn't understand these vampires.

"I don't work with others. If you want to give me the name of the vampire you want dead, I'll consider looking into things, but I don't want anything to do with your nest. I intended to tell Maciah that whenever he popped back up, but if you could just pass the information along, that'd be great."

She jutted her lower lip out. "For reals? Like there is no convincing you? Because I was seriously so excited about having another girl around. I mean, there's Nikki, but she's hardly ever home. I'm always stuck with men. I am so over them walking around like they're better than me just because I'm a woman. I could kill them all if I wanted, you know?"

Mother effer, she talked a lot.

"Then, why don't you?"

Rachel finally took a drink of her Bloody Mary, and I tried not to gag. Then, I was distracted by the fact that she held her pinky out while taking deep gulps until every drop was gone. These vamps were insane.

She wiped the sides of her lips with the drink napkin, then leveled her gaze on me. "Because I'm not a monster, Amersyn."

Her words were simple, but they rocked my core. I didn't know why. I shouldn't care. I killed vampires. Nothing more, nothing less. They were bloodsuckers that needed to be cleared from the history books.

And yet...

Rachel grinned at me, nearly bouncing in her seat as she reached for me. "Oh, oh, oh! You're actually considering the offer now. Maciah said I'd never get you to see reason, but us girls, we've got to stick together. He had no business breaking into your home like that. I'd told him so. I tried to get him to approach you like this, but no, that stubborn vampire never listens to reason, especially not when it comes to killing his creator."

She'd gone on another tangent, and while I'd nearly zoned out by the end, I hadn't missed what the vamp had let slip.

"What did you just say?" I asked.

"Oh, crap. Maciah is going to kill me."

6

VAMPIRES HAD VERY FEW LAWS AND EVEN FEWER THAT couldn't be broken. I'd done my research and knew a couple of them, like the one Rachel had just let slip. They couldn't kill their creator, and their creator couldn't kill them. It was the most asinine rule ever, but I'd never heard of a way around it.

"And given you haven't gone to do the task, I can assume Maciah's creator is also yours?" I asked carefully.

She sighed. "Well, the cat is out of the bag now. I might as well tell you everything, but not here. Can we go somewhere else?"

I didn't really want to go anywhere with the bloodsucker, but I was intrigued. Learning more about their inner workings excited me, especially now that I knew Dmitri and Rigo were from a bigger nest. Whatever I could get Rachel to tell me just might be invaluable.

"Fine." I waved down Dave, and he came right over. "I'm taking off for the night. I only stopped by to check on you and see if you heard anything about last night."

He laughed. "You're checking on me? Right. Well, come see me tomorrow. It should be a slower night, and I'll let you know what I've seen."

I didn't like the sound of that, but I trusted Dave enough. If there was something urgent, he wouldn't have kept me waiting, so it was probably nothing.

As I went to pay for my whiskey, Rachel beat me to it, laying a hundred-dollar bill on the counter, then winking at me. "Those bartenders are nice on the eyes. That alone deserves a good tip."

Oh, she was going to be a handful.

I pulled my keys out of my front pocket as we walked out of the door. "Where's your car? I'll follow you."

"I didn't bring a car. I was hoping I could ride with you, and we could maybe go somewhere you know. I'm not supposed to be here right now. You might not understand what I risked by coming to you, but it's important enough that I was willing to put my status within my nest on the line."

"Get in the car and don't touch a single thing," I snapped as I unlocked my Lexus.

Rachel let out a godawful squeal that had me instantly regretting my choices over the last few minutes. What was wrong with me? Two run-ins with a vampire that hadn't tried to kill me was all it took to suddenly have one in my car? I wasn't sure what to think. I had my rules, and I was breaking them. This would either lead to something great, or my demise.

She was in the front seat before I could take my words back. I took a deep breath as I slowly walked around to the driver's side. I could do this without killing her. I could figure out the information I needed and then be done with them.

Once I was in the car, Rachel beamed at me, brushing her long bangs behind her ear. "Can we go to your condo? It looked so nice from the outside."

If she was already aware of where I lived, I didn't see the harm in it. Plus, I'd already placed all of my stakes back where they belonged. I had more weapons there than I did in my car if things went in the wrong direction. Or maybe it was the right direction...

Rachel reached for the radio as I drove toward the interstate, and I snapped my fingers at her. "What did I say?"

"Seriously? I can't even turn on music? I thought we were going to be friends, Amersyn. You don't have to be so rude."

I slammed on my brakes, grateful nobody was behind me on the side street. "Let's get one thing straight. I am not your friend."

"But you could be," she interrupted. Again.

"And I don't like being cut off while I'm talking."

"Then maybe you should be nicer," she interjected.

I sneered at her. "Still wasn't done."

Rachel waved a hand for me to proceed, and I took

another deep breath, regretting the decision when her foul stench of decaying flesh entered my senses.

I was never going to survive this.

"We're not friends. You don't have permission to touch my things. I am not one of you. I kill monsters like you for breakfast, lunch, and dinner. Remember that before you piss me off again," I said, then pressed harder on the gas than necessary, skidding the tires.

"Oh, Amersyn. I like you," she said, not at all fazed by my words.

"That makes one of us," I muttered. I wasn't at all pleased with myself. I was letting these vampires get under my skin. I was breaking my own rules. And for what?

Vengeance that wasn't even guaranteed.

My fingers tightened around the steering wheel as I sped onto the interstate, toward the better parts of Portland.

Rachel stayed quiet the rest of the drive and I didn't have to stake her in my car. That would have required a trip to the detailers afterward that I didn't have time for.

When we arrived at the condos, I used my card to access the parking garage. Rachel drooled over the various sports cars from the other residents as I tried to tune her out. I got out of the car before she'd even unbuckled and headed for the bank of elevators.

A small gust of wind circled me, then she appeared by my side. "Not even going to wait for me, huh?"

"Seems you're here, so there was no need to wait."

There was already a waiting elevator and I walked right in, swiping my card for my floor and pressing the "close door" button. Rachel tsked at me before blurring inside and narrowly missed the doors biting her ass.

She tapped her stiletto heel and crossed her arms, staring at me.

I managed to ignore her—just barely—and sighed in relief when the ding sounded for my condo. My eyes searched the open area, checking for anything out of place and taking a deep inhale for recent scents that didn't belong.

Nothing stood out except the citrus scent still lingering from Maciah's earlier and unwanted visit. An odd choice in cologne, but it had worked for him.

Rachel's hands were clasped behind her back as she roamed my living room, then entered the kitchen. She managed not to touch a single thing and I was impressed.

"How many bedrooms and bathrooms?" she asked, moving toward the window view of the city.

"Three of each."

She glanced back at me, longing in her burnt-red eyes. "Oh, what I wouldn't give to have my own house."

"Right. Well, how about you start telling me more about this vampire creator?" I wasn't Rachel's friend. No matter how normal she seemed. All I needed was to take one deep breath to remind myself of that. The scent of dead human blood flowed through her veins.

"Am I allowed to sit?" she asked.

"Sure," I droned, following her to my living room. She lounged across the chaise at the end of my couch, and I took over the recliner, knowing there were stakes stashed in the arms.

"So, I know I slipped up earlier. You weren't supposed to know Silas is Maciah's creator, but now that you do, I still can't tell you anything about Maciah, but I can tell you about me."

I nodded. That would have to do, and then I could go my own way and figure out how to end more vampires in the process.

"So, I've been with Maciah for the last twenty-three years."

It was my turn to interrupt. "How old are you?"

"I'm technically forever twenty-five, but I've been walking this earth for forty-eight years. I was living my dream life before I was turned. I had the best friends, a kickass 1972 Challenger that made all the boys drool, and a small apartment overlooking a creek that I called my own."

There was a longing in her eyes that almost had me sympathizing with her. I wanted to smack myself as I did my best to remember she was a murderer.

"Aerosmith was playing just a few towns over from mine. They were one of my favorites. A few of my girlfriends scored tickets, and there was no way I could say no. We went together, dressed to the nines, and danced to the music as if our lives depended on it. Little did I know, in a way, mine did."

"How so?" I asked.

Rachel's body shuddered as she closed her eyes. "I'd needed to pee so badly. I'd tried to hold it. The show was almost over. I didn't want to miss the encore, but I couldn't wait any longer. I darted off to the bathrooms, running as quickly as I could in three-inch platform shoes. I'd never peed faster in my life as I heard the band start up again. When I exited the bathroom, I stupidly took an extra moment to stare up at the sky and sway to the music instead of hurrying back. Hands grabbed on to me, nails cut into my skin, and I tried to scream, but a second hand covered my mouth. His red eyes are something I'll never forget."

A lone tear fell down her cheek. Her eyes were still closed as she was lost in the memory. I couldn't prevent myself from feeling bad for her. Rachel didn't choose this life. Yet, I couldn't stop from thinking she'd had a choice. She didn't have to feed. She could have died. Instead, she'd chosen to kill and live.

Rachel continued, "Silas turned me into a vampire, then threw a card at me, stating I'd either find my way or I'd die. I didn't know what I'd become. I didn't know why my throat burned with a need I couldn't understand. Silas only wanted me if I was strong enough to kill. I didn't know that then, but I know it now. I was lucky, though. I never found my way into his nest."

"But you're not dead, either. What happened?" I tried to keep the disgust out of my voice. She would have only stayed alive because she fed, and a newborn vampire had very little control. She had to have killed someone from her thirst.

"Maciah found me as I was stalking a security guard. I didn't understand what I was doing, but I was hunting the innocent man until Zeke tackled me to the ground. I nearly tore the poor guy's eyes out as I fought against his hold. Then, Maciah shoved blood from a bag down my throat. He saved my life that day. He gave me a choice. The right choice. Some days, I wonder if I'd been better off dying, but I have a family now, and that means something to me."

Rachel sat up, drying her cheeks and meeting my stare. "Silas is still turning humans. He is still killing. We have tried to stop him, and for a while we thought we had, but he's resurfaced. When Maciah and Zeke found you, we finally had a solution to our problem: you."

Mother effing effer. I didn't want to help these people. I didn't want to see them as anything other than the monsters I'd always known vampires to be.

This Silas dude sounded like the worst of the worst. Rachel hadn't wanted this life. I knew she wasn't lying about that. Nobody could fake that kind of emotion.

Even still, I hesitated.

"We'll help you find Dmitri and Rigo. We're not tricking you. Maciah isn't that kind of man, and if you'd give him a chance, you'd see that for yourself," Rachel added.

Yeah, that was exactly what I was worried about.

7

I<small>T WAS ALMOST NINE BY THE TIME</small> R<small>ACHEL DIRECTED US TO</small> the vampire nest. I'd only ever been to crackhouse-looking bloodsucker hideouts. I wasn't sure what I expected from a vampire that showed up to my house in a suit, and I shouldn't have been surprised when it was a mansion, yet I was.

My Lexus fit in with the neighborhood of ginormous houses, plethora of trees separating the homes, and large fences keeping unwanted guests out. Well, maybe most guests. Likely not supernatural ones.

The walls around Maciah's property were steel-grey stucco with iron rods sticking out of the top, daring someone to try to jump over without having one end up in their ass. I pulled up to the gate, and there wasn't a keypad, only a screen.

Rachel was out of the car before I could ask what next. She pressed her palm over the glass surface, and the screen flashed white, then beeped twice. "Welcome, Second Best," the computer voice said.

"Freaking Zeke," she sneered, then glanced at me. "That's Maciah's other top vampire. He likes to think he's the best, but I've proved him wrong time and time again."

I just shook my head. These vampires were seeming more and more normal by the second. I didn't like it one bit.

As the gates parted, Rachel got back into my car and directed me to park in the roundabout. "If you come here for longer than a visit, we'll get you access to the garage. This beauty shouldn't be left to the elements."

She wasn't wrong about that. It was freezing in Portland this time of year. Snow flurries had been happening on and off the last week, and I preferred to keep my car under cover.

As I stared up at the massive house, I was once again second-guessing going there. I'd made a choice to stick with my rules, then I'd let Rachel change my mind. I'd let her show of humanity weaken my resolve. I didn't know what that meant for me, and that wasn't helping my mood.

At this point, I was winging things. A part of me was convinced I should help them. That it was the right thing to do and that they would be useful to my hunting. But the very core of who I was had been rocked. I was off kilter.

Rachel was already out of the car as I worked to get my head as right as it could be given the circumstances.

I patted my jacket pockets, double-checking my stakes were still present. With four on each side, plus new daggers inserted into my boots, I was as safe as I was going to be walking into the home of who-knew-how-many vampires.

That was probably something I should have asked before arriving.

After getting out, I scanned the yard and house. There were mature trees all around us, green manicured grass, and even rose bushes lining the house. So freakishly normal. The house was two, possibly three stories, given I could see windows that likely went to a daylight basement.

The outside was made from the same charcoal stucco as the fence with windows every six feet or so on both the lower and upper levels. Vampires usually weren't much for natural light, so that made no sense to me until I stepped inside.

There was the darkest tint ever over the glass as I turned to my left and right, checking for vampires. Rachel might have been nice, but I didn't trust whoever else lived with her.

To my left was a sitting area with bookshelves covering every available wall. On a coffee table, there was an antique map of the world I badly wanted to check out. Something about old maps always intrigued me. The world was ever-changing, and it was interesting to find countries that didn't exist anymore.

On the right where Rachel stood waiting for me was an open foyer with couches and two staircases leading to separate parts of the house. I tried to peer further ahead, but there was nothing other than closed doors.

"Maciah is waiting for us in his office. Come on," Rachel said with a smile.

I hesitated for the slightest of seconds before stepping forward. My chest tightened at the thought of seeing Maciah again. He was different. He called to something deeper inside me, and I didn't like it. I also hated that he thought I was one of them. There was nothing vampire about me. Not one tiny bit.

Rachel led the way up the right set of stairs. The wooden staircase was in perfect condition, without a chip or dent to be seen. My fingers trailed up the smooth surface as I followed the vampire. Okay, maybe this wouldn't be so bad. I could have the conversation. Get the information I needed and leave. Easy as that.

Those thoughts were only wishful thinking as laughter sounded from the left side of the house. "Dude, did you see him? He was so scared. It was almost too easy," one male vampire said, likely bragging about his newest kill.

Without hesitation, I pulled a stake from my jacket and aimed for the murderer. Just as I moved my arm forward, Rachel grabbed on to my wrist. "Listen before you act, Amersyn."

I snarled at her as I tried to pull out of her grip, but she was strong, and I was curious what she meant.

"Right! I can't believe the newbie is scared of bunnies. A vampire afraid of little fluffy animals. He's going to fit right in here," the other guy said as they disappeared into a different section of the house.

"Our vampires like to torment…but not the way you think. We just saved another newborn from the hands of the vampires you hunt. This one is only sixteen. The youngest we've found. He's a good kid, and we're going to take care of him, because that's what we do here."

I put the stake away, my mind reeling. Those vampires were more like frat guys playing games on the new pledges. I wanted to see them as monsters, but Rachel was making it harder than I liked.

My foundations were being rocked and spinning inside my head. Not knowing what to believe anymore wasn't helping. If there were good vampires like there were shifters and witches, then what did that mean for me as a hunter? The fact that I didn't have the answer grated on my nerves.

"Great. Let's keep going then," I said with more snark than she deserved.

Rachel grinned at me. "I'll wear you down. We're meant to be friends, and I'm going to make sure that happens."

"Please don't," I deadpanned.

Rachel reached for me, then thought better of it. "Baby steps. I can handle that. I've got all the time in the world."

Without any other distractions, we continued through the house. There were old paintings hanging on the walls, but no photos, which I thought was weird.

I half-expected a shrine of some kind, yet there was nothing of the sort.

Rachel rattled off random facts about where some of the art came from, but I had no interest. Not until she said we'd arrived at Maciah's office.

The door was cracked open, and she pushed the wooden door further into the room before entering ahead of me.

I paused, reminding myself of who I was.

I was Amersyn Holt. Vampire hunter. My mission was to end the lives of those who stole the three most important people in the world to me. Nothing else mattered. Not even these odd-acting vampires or their problems.

I was there for information, not to make friends or sympathize with them.

A means to an end. Nothing more, nothing less.

While walking into the room, I did a quick scan, checking for an ambush before I focused on the details. The walls were a sage green, and the ceiling was more of an eggshell color, making the office appear lighter than it was with the wood shutters covering the windows.

There were recessed lights above us. Maciah currently stood behind a large wooden desk. The vampire I'd stabbed with a blade the other night sat on a brown leather couch with his legs crossed, glaring at me.

Rachel had stayed by the door, closing it behind me once I fully entered the room.

She looped her arm through mine, causing me to flinch at her closeness. "I told you I would win her over."

Zeke barked out a laugh. "She looks like she wants to poke both of your eyes out."

"For now," Rachel replied confidently. She was going to be a hard one to shake.

Maciah stepped around his desk. He was wearing light-grey slacks and another white dress shirt, but this time the sleeves were rolled halfway up his forearms, revealing muscles I had no business noticing.

"Amersyn." He greeted me as if we were well-known acquaintances.

"Vampire," I said in return. It would be better if I didn't use their names. Names were too personable.

"So, have you decided to take my offer?" he asked, sticking his hands in his pockets and drawing my attention south.

Damn, this was not good.

I met his eyes. "You mean the offer to kill your creator because you're unable to? I'm considering it, but I wanted to hear it from you. You can't kill Silas. You need me."

Fiery eyes narrowed on Rachel who held her left hand up. "She was going to find out soon enough. I didn't tell her anything else about you. Just me. And she's here, so I don't want any crap over doing what needed to be done."

"Out. Both of you," Maciah said to his vampires as he casually leaned against the front of his desk.

Zeke eyed me but addressed his leader. "Are you sure?"

Maciah didn't bother to look or answer the other vampire. A second later, Zeke was off the couch and headed out the door. Rachel winked at me, then whispered, "Give him hell."

Who were these people?

Maciah sighed as the door closed once more, leaving me alone with the vampire.

"You lied to me," I said first.

"No, I omitted. Completely different. I told you, I don't lie."

I didn't believe that for one moment. "Right. Glad to know we're making up our own rules."

I crossed my arms and leaned against the wall near the door. I didn't want to get any closer to the vampire than necessary.

"Do I bother you?" he asked, seeming amused.

"Yes, you do."

He tilted his head. "How so?"

I opened my mouth to name off a laundry list of things, but nothing came out as quickly as I wanted. "You're a vampire and reek of blood that doesn't belong to you," I finally said, though that last bit was a lie. He didn't smell of decaying flesh like most vampires. The citrus scent coming from him was tangy and alluring and overpowering. I didn't know why and didn't want to care, either. I couldn't care about anything when it came to this man.

"It infuriates you that I'm not the monster you

wanted me to be," he stated, seeming so sure he knew my thoughts even though he didn't know me.

Yet, he wasn't wrong.

"You still drink blood. You might save other vampires, but you're still a bloodsucker," I spat, trying to find the anger I'd need to keep my resolve from softening toward this group of people.

"I don't drink from the tap, Amersyn. Any blood consumed by me and my vampires is purely donated by well-compensated donors and stored in bags, not fresh bodies." Maciah stepped closer to me, inhaling.

"You do that often," I said, holding my ground.

"Do what, Amersyn?" He took another step.

"Smell the air. Why?"

"Only around you," he replied without answering me.

"Why?" I repeated.

He was within inches of me, and I was trapped against the wall. My fingers itched to reach for a stake. I could end him. He was alone, and I was armed. It would be so simple.

"Because your blood calls to me like nothing I have ever scented in my nearly eight decades of life." Maciah leaned in closer, his breath warm against my skin.

My body trembled, but not from fear.

Bloodsucker. Bloodsucker. Bloodsucker, I repeated in my mind, trying to stop picturing him naked.

His palms pressed against the wall behind me. "I told you, I don't lie, Amersyn. The truth will always leave my lips. It is now and it was back at your condo."

That last bit grated on my nerves, killing the growing tension between us. "Just because you believe something is true doesn't make it so."

He grinned, taking a step back. "You're right, but the same applies to you as well. Maybe we'll both learn something in this little partnership of ours."

"You said my blood calls to you. What does that mean?" I asked.

He chuckled and turned away from me. "You're not ready for that answer, Amersyn."

Maciah's words made me see red. He acted so sure of himself and like he knew me better than I knew myself. The cocky prick was driving me mad with mixed emotions. I might not kill him, but I had no problem showing him what I was capable of.

I shoved off the wall, launching myself at him, pulling out a dagger from my boot as I did so. He turned just as I swiped at his ribs, ruining another one of his precious dress shirts he seemed so fond of.

Maciah's fingers wrapped around my wrist, squeezing. "Let go," he demanded.

"Not a damn chance." I brought my knee up, but he blocked my move and I hit his thigh instead of his junk where I was aiming.

"You have no idea what I've been through. There isn't anything I can't handle," I seethed, yanking my arm from his hold and taking another swing at him.

Maciah blurred, appearing behind me and pulling both of my hands behind my back. "The truth is always more than any of us can handle. I know from

82

experience," he whispered against my ear, sending chills down my spine.

I threw my head backward, finally catching him off guard, and cracked his nose. He let go of me, but only for a moment.

"That was rude," he hissed, pressing me against the wall behind us.

The dagger was still in my hand between us. One move and I could stab him. His eyes stared down at me, daring me to do so.

"What are you waiting for, Amersyn?" he taunted.

When I didn't move or respond, he took the blade from my grip and threw it behind us. I had no idea where it landed, and I no longer cared. Maciah's breath mixed with my own as he inched closer and closer to me.

"Do you really believe you can handle the truth?" he murmured, his fingers brushing strands of my hair away from my face before he gripped my neck possessively.

"I do," I nearly panted like a fool.

"Then, I won't keep it from you." He paused and inhaled once more before speaking again. "You are a vampire, Amersyn. The daughter of the last original vampire and a royal heir. One that I am bound to protect."

8

MACIAH'S STATEMENT HAD SEARED MY HEART LIKE A declaration of truth, causing me to flinch back as if he'd slapped me instead of whispered words of certainty and protection.

"I think you drank some tainted blood. I am none of those things, I assure you," I said, trying not to be the bitch I really wanted to be. Normally, that was my way of deflecting, but trying to avoid this subject was clearly not going to happen.

Maciah reached for me again, but I sidestepped him. There was no way I was going to be able to think clearly if I allowed that.

"I've been tracking you for days. I scented your blood two weeks ago. I don't know who you fought or how you were injured, but I was near enough to smell you. I haven't been able to stop ever since."

No. No. No. This could not be happening.

Maciah continued, "I've been spending every night

searching Portland and learning whatever I could about you. When I saw those vampires ready to kill you, I nearly lost my mind. I could smell your blood again, and I knew you were hurt. I just wanted to make sure you were okay. Then, I saw what you were capable of, and I confirmed what I'd known from the start, but tried not to believe. It was clear to me that you weren't a woman needing saving, and if I was going to get close to you, I had to find a reason for you to trust me."

"So, you used my need to avenge my family?" I said with little emotion. I was riding a fine line between wanting to murder him and finding his attempts to win me over endearing. The former was winning.

"Listen, Amersyn. I know this seems wrong and not at all possible, but I am telling you the truth."

Damn it, why did I want to believe him so badly?

"Your mother is your mother, and before she met your father, she fell in love with Darius Saint. The last living original vampire. The only of our kind that was capable of creating natural-born vampires. For years, he remained elusive. Moving from place to place. He was stronger than us all, but he merely wanted to be left alone. Then, he met your mother. He fell in love—"

I cut him off. "Vampires don't love. They murder and steal and harm."

I expected Maciah to snarl at me, but instead, he showed me pity. Something I didn't want from him. Not one effing bit.

"Not all of us chose this life, Amersyn. Darius was born into a world that he wanted nothing to do with.

His brothers were killed off one by one, and he just wanted to know peace. In the end, he did with your mother. Then, she became pregnant and everything changed. The moment he found out you were going to exist, he knew his time was over."

I began to pace as I tried to put together Maciah's asinine story. It couldn't possibly be the truth, but at the same time, in my heart, I couldn't continue to deny his words. My mother had always said the world was a darker place than many knew. That we had to be prepared for anything. I'd always thought she meant another world war or an epidemic. Not anything straight out of a fantasy novel.

A part of me was hurt that she'd never told me the truth, or at least that the monsters were real. Then again, maybe she'd just never had the chance. Unfortunately, I'd never know for sure.

"Do you want me to continue?" Maciah asked.

I glared at him, stopping in front of his desk. This would be so much easier if he was an asshole, but no. He was being understanding and nice, and that infuriated me beyond no end.

I waved a hand. "Yeah, whatever."

He fought a smile, moving to his desk and searching for something while he spoke. "Before Darius died, he called a favor in to a witch. He asked her to conceal who you were for as long as you were mortal."

"So, I'm not a vampire?" I interrupted.

Maciah barely glanced at me. "I didn't say that. I called you mortal. There's a difference between that and being human." He continued to search through his desk, and I went back to pacing.

"What was this witch's name?" I asked.

He kneeled on the ground, checking a filing cabinet. "I don't know. I only have pieces of the story that I've put together over the years."

"Why? Why did you care what Darius did?" I asked.

Maciah ignored me, so I went around his desk. Just as I was about to jerk him up by the back of his head, he glanced up at me, a gleam in his eyes.

"Darius saved me once, and I made him a promise. I didn't know about you then. I didn't know about you, in particular, until I first smelled your blood. Everyone had always thought Darius had a son, and if anyone figures out that your brother wasn't the heir, you're not going to be safe."

A vice tightened around my chest, pressing in on me until I could barely breathe. "Are you saying my baby brother died because someone thought he was me?"

The world around me was coming undone. I couldn't... No, this couldn't be true. I couldn't be responsible for their deaths.

Suddenly, Maciah's hands were cupping my face gently, yet firm enough to keep me from collapsing onto the floor like I wanted. "This is not your fault, Amersyn. I don't know how they found your mother or how anyone knew about you—"

"You knew about me," I pointed out.

"Because I was your father's friend, but even then, I knew very little until recently." He moved one hand to my waist and reached for a book he'd set on his desk with the other. "This will tell you more about who you are and what you come from. Not all of it is pretty, but each of us can choose to be better. Darius proved that. He was a good man. You should be proud he was your father."

I was supposed to be proud that a *vampire* was my father? How in the world was I supposed to do that?

Maciah pushed the book toward me, but I couldn't stand the thought of touching the leather-bound pages. I didn't want to be a monster. I couldn't be the one thing I hated most in this world.

Panic was clawing its way through me. I wanted to scream. I wanted to cry. I wanted to kill something.

"How do you know my brother wasn't the heir? Why do you believe it's me?" I asked.

"Because I am drawn to you, Amersyn. There is magic in your blood. Magic that can't exist in a human. Your scent brought me to my knees the first time I sensed you. Nothing in my many years has ever done that."

Damn it, why did I find that so hot? Maciah was staring down at me with a softness in his muddy-red eyes I'd never seen in the vampires I'd crossed paths with.

His fingers stroked my ribs where he still held me, and we were only inches apart. My world had been shattered, and his touch was the only thing keeping me from falling apart.

Maciah's eyes roamed over my face as our bodies

gravitated closer. I could barely breathe as I tried to figure out what was happening. He said he was bound to protect me, that the draw to me brought him to his knees.

I wanted to call him a liar. I wanted to jab a stake through his heart and pretend our conversation never happened. More than all that, I wanted his lips on mine.

Maciah set the book back down, and his hand reached around until his fingers disappeared into my thick ebony locks. "You need to quit looking at me like that, Amersyn."

"Or what?" I breathed.

His hold on my hair increased. "Or this."

Maciah closed the distance between us. His lips pressed against mine, surprisingly soft and warm, and not what I expected. There was a hesitation on his part, waiting for me to push him away, but I couldn't. I didn't want to. That alone should have made me run in the opposite direction. Instead, I pressed closer to the vampire and threw all rational thought out the window.

A rumble built in his chest as I opened my mouth to him, and the hard muscles of his tall frame warmed every inch of my body. I dug my nails into his shoulders, tearing his dress shirt with the force of my grip.

Our teeth and tongues clashed in a dance I never wanted to end. A moan slipped from my lips, and Maciah's lips traveled down my neck. My head tilted to the side, allowing him more room to devour me, and then…I froze.

The sharp edges of Maciah's teeth scraped against my skin. An action that I wouldn't have thought twice about if he was human, but he wasn't. The man was a vampire. A blood-drinking creature of the night.

I was a hunter. Someone who'd sworn to kill every vampire she could.

Okay, maybe that wasn't exactly what I was anymore. I mostly believed Maciah wasn't lying to me, but that didn't mean the foundations of who I was at heart had changed.

They couldn't have. I still had vampires to kill. I had a family to avenge and other humans to protect.

I'd given in to the desire Maciah had evoked within me. I'd been weak, and I couldn't allow it to happen again.

Maciah sensed the stiffness in my body and slowly lifted his head, stroking my cheek as he searched my face for answers. "What's wrong?"

I sighed. I wanted to be cruel. It was what I should do so that he would leave me the hell alone, but instead, I gently pushed him away from me and took a step back.

"It's been a long couple of days. I have a lot to think about, and I'd like to do that alone," I said.

Hurt crossed his face as a crease formed between his brows. "Okay. We have rooms—"

"No, Maciah. I have a home of my own with rooms. I'm going there." I took several steps toward the door, needing more space between us before I lost my resolve.

His face hardened, and gone was the gentle man I'd just been pressed against. "My number is in your phone. Call me when you have more questions. And take this." He reached for the book and handed it to me.

I once again hesitated to take it, but Maciah had already been more forthcoming than I could have ever expected. I didn't want to insult him further. That thought also made me want to punch myself in the throat. I wasn't supposed to care what vampires thought.

Regardless, I took the book and turned for the door. As my fingers gripped the handle, I sensed Maciah come closer.

"Please, be safe," he murmured.

I nodded, wanting desperately to look back at him, but my pride wouldn't allow it. The door opened, and I put one foot in front of the other, ignoring the eyes of other vampires around me as I headed toward the front door.

9

MY KNUCKLES WERE WHITE AS I DROVE MY CAR WITHOUT knowing where I was going. I couldn't breathe. I was losing control. Nothing in my world was what I thought.

I didn't want to believe Maciah, but my gut was rarely wrong. The book he'd given me sat in my passenger's seat, mocking me. I was what I hated most in the world.

How could fate be so cruel?

As I sat at a red light, I closed my eyes and took several deep inhales and exhales. I was still Amersyn Holt. Maciah had said I was mortal, which meant I wasn't technically a vampire. I needed to know when that change was supposed to come.

Someone honked behind me, and I flipped them off as I sped ahead, turning randomly left and right until I was at the edge of Portland. I parked and side-eyed the book.

Mother-effing vampire.

The time on my dashboard said it was almost midnight, which meant I'd been driving aimlessly for close to two hours. I reached for the leather cover. I could do this. I'd been through worse. I wasn't a vampire yet. Maybe there was a way to prevent that from happening.

My fingers had barely brushed over the faded text when my phone dinged. I didn't believe in coincidences, so I tossed the book into the back seat and looked at my phone.

Dave: We should chat sooner rather than later. Don't come inside. Text me when you arrive.

Me: Be there in ten.

This was a distraction I could work with. The book I was happily going to ignore a little while longer might have answers, but as Maciah kindly pointed out, maybe I wasn't ready for them.

I loved who I was. I loved what I stood for. I loved ridding the world of monsters. I didn't want anything to change. This was in my blood. It was what I was meant to do—kill vampires.

As my foot pressed down on the accelerator, I decided right then that nothing was going to change. My DNA might not be what I thought, but I was still me. Whatever Maciah thought he was protecting me from wasn't necessary.

I'd fought and killed supernatural murderers for five years, and I'd do that for another fifty if fate allowed it to be.

The later the night got, the lighter traffic became, and I was at Crossroads within seven minutes. I texted Dave that I'd parked in the alley a block away. The same one where I'd been ambushed by the five vampires and where I'd first seen Maciah and Zeke.

My eyes scanned the shadows, remembering how the two of them had jumped in to help me without a second thought. Maciah said he was bound to protect me, that my blood called to him, but what did that mean? As far as I knew, vampires didn't have mates like shifters did.

Was there another reason I was attracted to Maciah? Shit. Maybe I needed to take a look at the book sooner rather than later.

I reached for it, but Dave opened the passenger door before I could grasp the aged cover. He was glancing around, and his hands had a slight shake to them.

"What's going on, Dave?" I asked. Very little rattled this human. He worked in a damn supernatural bar. Sure, he had a slight immunity with the protection of Chester Dean behind him, but Dave had been fearless since the first day I met him.

"There were vampires in the bar asking about a hunter." His voice was low, even though we were enclosed in the car.

"Me specifically?" I asked.

He shook his head. "They wanted the best, which I normally would have said was you, but something about this crew wasn't right. Their eyes had black rings around a dark crimson color, and their skin was like stone. These were old and powerful vampires, Am."

"Are they still there?" Maybe I could sneak in through the back and get a look at them myself.

"No, they left before I texted you. They said they had a problem that needed to be dealt with. I panicked and gave them Simon's phone number. Shit, Amersyn. I don't know if that was the right thing to do or not, but something about them isn't right. They asked a lot of questions."

Simon was a solid hunter, but he was only ever out for himself, which was why I never worked with him, not even on the easiest of jobs. He'd take the contract from these vampires, whatever it was.

"What kind of questions?" I asked.

Dave scanned the alley and then behind us again. His breathing was picking up, and I rested a hand on his shoulder. "Dave, you reached out to me for a reason. You're okay. Do you want me to take you to Steve?"

"No. No, I'm fine. I don't know why I'm acting like this." Dave's hands rubbed over his face as he tried to regain control of his emotions.

"What about earlier when I was there? How about we back up a few hours?" I suggested.

"Yeah, I mostly just wanted to make sure you were okay. You were pretty messed up last night, Amersyn. Where did you go?"

That singular question made me tense up. Dave never asked where I went. I took into consideration he was having a shit night, but still, suddenly I was a little less trusting of the bartender.

"I went somewhere, and as you can see, I'm fine now," I answered curtly.

He muttered to himself before apologizing. "Sorry. I know your rules. It's just these vampires. Maybe they did something to me."

I grabbed his wrist. "Tell me what happened."

He took a steadying breath and met my gaze. "One of them wouldn't leave the bar. He wanted my constant attention. He asked the most questions, too, like how many hunters came to the bar? How often? How many of them were women and how many men? What type of weapons your kind carried and average group size of a hunter party? At first, I'd thought they were trying to hire someone. By then, I'd already given them Simon's number, but this one kept on, repeating questions in different ways, almost as if he was trying to trip me up. Each one only made me think more of you, and I didn't know what else to do."

"What do you mean by that, Dave?" I asked calmly, even though I wanted to scream.

"I told them if Simon wasn't what they were looking for, then maybe I could find them another hunter, but I didn't say your name. I just wanted the creep to leave me alone. I swear, Amersyn. I'd never do anything to put you in danger on purpose." Dave was near tears.

Damn it. What was happening to my world?

I released my hold on him, not trusting myself to keep from hurting him on accident. "It's okay. I appreciate you telling me. Did any of them tell you their names?"

"I didn't get any of their names, but one of them mentioned a guy named Viktor a couple of times. Though, he wasn't present. He sounded more like a boss they were following orders from. Does that help?"

My blood ran cold. I'd killed Viktor already. Maybe it wasn't the same one. Yeah, it had to be someone else. He was one of my first kills, the first in the group of five I'd been able to track down just south of Portland in Salem. These vampires weren't after me. I was safe.

Then, realization hit me like a freight train.

Mother-effing effer.

I never saw Viktor turn to dust.

I stabbed him through the chest. I used the right stake. He should have died, but was I absolutely certain? Not anymore.

One of his vampires had tackled me off Viktor right after I'd staked him. I'd thought he'd turned to dust before I had the chance to kill the other one, but maybe he hadn't. Maybe he'd run off and I'd made the biggest of rookie mistakes that was now back to bite me in the ass.

"Does that help, Am?" Dave repeated his earlier question.

I nodded stiffly. "You need to stay away from these vampires, Dave. I don't know anything about them, but I'm going to figure it out. If they come back, you text me right away. Don't wait until after they've left. Do you understand?"

"What if I'm right and they're looking for you?" he asked.

"Don't worry about that. I'll find them first," I replied, and Dave nodded, but he didn't seem sure about that. Whoever this group was, they'd shaken Dave in the worst way.

"Why don't you go home?" I suggested to him. He would be worthless behind the bar as he was.

"What are you going to do? I know it's none of my business, but I care about you, Amersyn. I don't want to see you get hurt. You're the only one that comes to that shithole of a bar that I think even has a soul anymore. The world needs you to stay alive."

I didn't want to think of Dave as my friend, because that made him a vulnerability, but damn if he wasn't one of the kindest people I'd ever met.

I grabbed his hand, giving it a firm and hopefully reassuring squeeze. "I'm going to be fine, Dave. Just watch your back and let me know what you hear. I'll probably keep away from Crossroads for a few days."

He nodded, seeming to take my absence from the bar as a sign I'd be more careful. "What about the brunette vamp from earlier? Did you kill her?"

The answer to that should have been yes. I killed nearly all vampires I came into contact with outside of the bar, but killing Rachel hadn't been something I'd done nor planned to do.

"She isn't going to be a problem," I said to Dave, letting him take that however he wanted.

He moved to open the door, then turned back to me. "Please, be safe."

I felt like people had been telling me to "be safe" a lot lately. With all the bombs being dropped in my lap, maybe it was time I took them seriously.

Dave was out of the car and hurrying back toward the bar before I could reply. I reversed far enough out of the alley to watch that he got safely back inside. Hopefully, Steve was coming to pick him up and I wouldn't need to worry about the shaken bartender.

I decided since my night had basically gone to shit that it was time to go back to my condo. Soon, I'd need to figure out what to do about my safehouse. Maciah knew where I was staying, and that made it no longer safe. Even if he didn't have intentions of hurting me, I still wanted somewhere I could go where no one would find me.

That was a protection I needed.

As I drove the roads on autopilot, I tried not to allow myself to lose sight of what needed to be done. My night hadn't gone how I could have ever predicted, but I was a skilled hunter. I knew what I had to do.

First, I needed to read over the book currently lying in my back seat. Second, I needed to remember who I was, no matter what the book said. Third, I had to figure out which problems were my biggest, so I'd know where to start.

I was going to keep a list, so that I stayed on track and focused on the things I was capable of doing. Everything would be fine.

Ha! Famous last words, I thought as I turned into the condo parking garage.

I watched the city grow smaller while the elevator took me up to my condo. My mental list was already started and growing as I considered outside influences. Nothing was unrealistic, just time consuming—and time was something I wasn't sure I had a lot of.

With the book in hand and my hunting bag on my other shoulder, I strode into my apartment, eager to start making progress, but I was stopped in my tracks.

Rachel lounged across my loveseat, still dressed in her one-piece suit, and had her stilettos crossed over one another.

"You didn't say goodbye," she grumbled, unmoving.

"You weren't invited in," I retorted.

She shushed me. "We're friends, Amersyn. That means the invite is always open."

"We. Are. Not. Friends," I said slowly and clearly, hoping she'd get the point. I might not want to kill her, but there also weren't any slumber parties in our future.

She nodded to the book finally, getting up. "So, you believe Maciah?"

"That's none of your business." I moved around her and toward my bedroom. Moving had officially been pushed to the top of my list.

Rachel laughed. "You're hilarious. Seriously, though. Let me help you. I've read that thing ten times since Maciah found out you existed."

Nope. Not happening. I wasn't working with a

vampire to figure out how I might turn into one. No way in hell. I narrowed my eyes and whirled around to face Rachel and tell her just what I thought.

She was standing just a foot behind me, eyes wide and full of care. There was nothing sinister about her, and she was making things really effing hard for me.

Damn it. I was going to regret this.

I pointed to the couch she'd just been on. "Sit or lay there. Don't say a word unless I ask you a question. Don't touch my stuff. If you can do all three of those things, then you can stay. For a very short period of time."

Rachel jumped up and down as she opened her mouth and let out a tiny squeal of excitement. I sneered at her, and she quickly shut her lips together, holding her hands up and backing away.

Smart vampire.

10

MY EYES BURNED AS THE HOURS PASSED, AND I BEGAN skimming the book instead of reading every word. I'd learned a lot about vampires, but not a ton that I hadn't already assumed or heard from Maciah. What I was searching for most hadn't appeared on the pages yet, and I was growing frustrated.

I paced the open space between the dining table and living room while reading. Rachel was still laying on the couch. Her eyes were closed, but I didn't for one moment think she was asleep.

Hope was thinning as the pages lessened. I'd thought there would be something to help solidify things for me. Like a bright light that made everything make sense.

Nothing of the sort happened.

Not until I turned another page and saw the final chapter heading: Original Heirs.

My chest eased when I would have expected the

opposite. This was supposedly what I was. An heir to one of the original monsters let loose on our earth. This was where I would find my answers.

The ten original vampire heirs, all male, were born to be immortal, but that doesn't mean they are immune to death. No one being is meant to live forever, but our legacy can. Each of the ten sons will create their own heirs with a bonded human. This human will be strong of mind and body. She will breed the strongest legacies for our kind and be cherished above all else for the lives she creates.

I paused, taking a breath. This book was written by vampires that didn't kill humans. Whoever wrote this saw their kind as Gods, which was hard to accept. A vampire cherishing a human was hard to picture.

The children born will be human like their mother until such a time that their mortal life ends. Then, they will return to their strongest form and live the immortal life gifted to them by their father.

So, I could grow old, and it still didn't matter. I'd somehow magically revert to a younger age where I was strong and capable to begin life as a vampire. Great. Super effing great.

Heirs will acquire abilities as they grow in their human body, but their true potential won't be unlocked until they've died and drank their first glass of blood.

Glass of blood? Not drink from a human? Where were these vampires, and why did they start massacring humans when this book made the originals sound like saints?

Then I snorted, remembering the original vampires' last name was Saint. Fitting.

Rachel turned her head toward me, watching, but still not saying anything. I really wanted to hate her. Really freaking badly.

I continued reading, and it was exactly as Maciah had said. I was the heir of an original. The witch hadn't given me enhanced abilities. She probably only lessened them so that I didn't stand out. I wanted to search for her and demand more answers, but I decided she'd done me a favor. I wouldn't have been ready to know who I was then.

I wasn't even sure I was ready now, but I could handle it. The only thing I didn't know was how the original vampires died. The book had conveniently left that part out. As I kept reading, my hope was that I'd live a long life just as I saw fit, and when I died, I could have a plan to end my immortal life, never having to stay a vampire for long.

The last section of the Original Heirs chapter was called Bonded Protectors, and I wanted to throw the book down and be done. I didn't want to know this part. Maciah had already expressed how he felt, but I wanted no part of it…even if I'd kissed him as if my life depended on it.

"Read it, Amersyn. You need to know," Rachel said softly, still sitting on the couch.

I snarled at her for being right, then continued.

Should an heir be in danger, a protector will be assigned to them. A vampire worthy of our most precious children will be bound to protect the heir with their own life. A bond will form between the two, strengthening a relationship that will last a lifetime.

This does not normally mean a romantic relationship, as the male heirs will only be able to create new life with chosen female humans. We need our children to thrive and keep our legacy alive. If there are no originals left to walk this earth, our legacy will end, and our kind will become something the world isn't prepared for. We cannot allow this to happen.

As I read the last few paragraphs, I realized there was no mention of female heirs, as if they'd never existed before. Maciah had mentioned that the vampires who attacked my family assumed my brother to be Darius's heir, but if I was reading this correctly, they'd been wrong only because I wasn't supposed to exist.

I glanced at Rachel. She was sitting up, waiting patiently for me to speak. "This is about more than killing Silas, isn't it?" I asked.

"It didn't start that way, and I don't think it will end that way, either. Though, he is a problem to be dealt with," she answered, calmer than normal.

Viktor, Silas, and being a vampire were my top three problems. I also had to consider what it meant that I was a female heir and how I was supposed to navigate this protector relationship with Maciah.

"This book is older than dirt, right?" I asked, and she nodded. "Have there been any other female heirs before me?"

Rachel shook her head. "Not that we know of.

Maciah made friends with Darius before the original met your mother. Darius saved him from Silas and showed him the old ways of vampires, telling him stories of how we used to live in peace with the humans. This is what Maciah is trying to bring back.

"Darius was the last original heir left. His nine brothers and all of their children had been hunted and killed. Vampires with the taste for human flesh rebelled against their creators and found ways to end their existence by working together to eliminate them, one by one."

"How did Darius die?" I asked, because it seemed like something I needed to know.

Rachel's lip downturned. "Are you sure you don't want to wait on some of this? You've already learned a lot tonight."

The vampire was concerned for me. That was an odd thing to see and believe. I was trying not to doubt her sincerity. She'd done nothing to deserve my distrust. If I considered the woman before me a monster just because of her makeup, that made me just as bad as the bloodsuckers I hunted. I needed to remember that, even if I didn't like it.

"I need to know, Rachel," I said, sure of my choice.

"Darius volunteered his life to save yours. Rumors had begun to circle that the last heir had found his breeder. Harsh description, I know, but that wasn't how Darius saw your mother. When he learned they were coming for him, he beat them to it. Your mother was already pregnant. He did the only thing he could think of to keep the two of you safe."

"He sacrificed himself," I said, already seeing where this was going.

Rachel nodded. "He was centuries old and tired of fighting. Very few vampires supported the old ways, or at least would speak out about their beliefs. He went to the group hunting him and told them he was tired of living alone. That he hadn't found his breeder as people had thought, and he was ready to give up. Darius was old and very convincing. The group bought it and publicly executed him."

Pain struck my chest for a man I'd never met. For someone I wasn't even supposed to care about. A vampire. My father.

"Why didn't he fight? Aren't originals supposed to be the strongest of your kind?" I asked.

"He could have fought, but at what cost? He had little support in our world. Darius did what he thought was best at the time, and I can't say I blame him. You shouldn't, either."

Between Rachel and the book, I'd been given a lot to consider. I wasn't sure what I was supposed to do next.

"So, now what? I'm the last heir. Someone figured out I still exist and they're after me, which created the bond Maciah feels toward me?" I asked, making sure I understood the situation correctly.

"It's more than a bond, Amersyn. It's an instinct Maciah can't ignore. The moment he scented you, his purpose changed. He knows exactly who you are to him, and he'd lay his life down for you. Maybe take that into consideration before you play with his heart."

My head shook. The book had said the bond between heir and protector wasn't a romantic one. Maciah wasn't supposed to feel anything toward me outside of a sense of duty, and I said as much to Rachel.

She grinned. "Oh, girl. How can you be so smart, yet so one-sided? Maciah doesn't want you because he's been chosen as your protector. He wants you because you're *you*."

Could I say the same? Did I feel drawn to Maciah because a deeper part of me knew he was there to keep me safe, or because he was sexy as sin and could kiss like nobody's business?

Rachel reached for me, grabbing on to my arm and pulling me from the chair I'd finished reading the book in. "Come on. You've had information overload. Let's watch a chick flick and get your mind off all this."

"I think I'm just going to go to bed." I knew she wanted us to be friends, but there wasn't much I enjoyed besides killing vampires. There wasn't a point in getting close to her.

She sighed, dragging me toward the couch. "You might think we're different, but I want the same things as you do. Our whole nest does."

"You want to expunge vampires from the earth?" I asked.

She grinned at me. "If that's truly what you wanted, I'd already be dead."

11

AFTER STARING MINDLESSLY AT THE CEILING, TRYING TO come to grips with everything I'd learned since meeting Maciah, I finally fell asleep around four that morning. When I awoke, I hoped the new day would have me in a better mood.

There were no unwanted guests in my condo, and I wasn't craving blood. I was just a normal twenty-one-year-old who hunted vampires, enjoying her whiskey-enhanced coffee while gazing over the city from her million-dollar home. Yep, totally normal.

Maciah didn't have all the information I'd hoped he would. We needed to figure out what brought Silas back into the game and why Viktor may or may not have resurfaced, and how much any of those answers had to do with Maciah becoming my protector. Then, maybe I could better understand what this all meant.

As I stood at the window thinking about working with the vampires, an excitement filled me that I didn't expect. Rachel was more than I expected. I couldn't deny that. I liked her enough. Maciah, though? I didn't know what to do about that situation.

I'd never been a fan of leading people on. I preferred to say things as they were instead of beating around the proverbial bush. The hard part about doing so with Maciah was that he only thought I was kidding myself.

Maybe I had been, but I knew who I was. I knew my purpose in this world. Knowing who my sperm donor was and having a magically bound protector wasn't going to change that. Not ever.

What I really needed to worry about was Viktor and the possibility that I hadn't killed him a few years ago. I considered reaching out to Simon, but he'd see through whatever reason I came up with. Everyone knew I worked alone, and any changes would draw attention. I had to be careful.

There was a chance this wasn't the same Viktor—I was sure there were plenty of vampires with that name —but my gut was screaming that wasn't the case here. I'd been new at hunting when I'd happened upon him. Too eager and too emotional. I'd acted without proper training.

After five years of hunting under my belt, I knew better. The next time I saw Viktor, I'd make sure he was nothing more than ash floating in the wind.

My stomach growled, distracting me from murderous thoughts. My house was only stocked with coffee, whiskey, random frozen foods not suitable for breakfast, and canned goods I could survive off if I was in hiding. But I wasn't, so I wanted real food. Like bacon. Yeah, I needed steaming hot French toast and a full plate of bacon.

I finished off my coffee, enjoying the buzz from the caffeine before heading out the door. Then, I remembered it was only twenty degrees out, so I doubled back and grabbed my favorite hoodie I'd bought in Montana. Warmest sweatshirt ever.

I even made sure my boots carried a couple of stakes and blades in case anyone had found out where I was. A hunter could never be too careful.

By the time I got to the garage, I was already feeling better. Whatever was in my DNA didn't matter. I wasn't going to let this new information stress me out. With a grin on my face, I unlocked my car as it came into view.

My smile fell, and I instantly regretted not slipping a stake up my sleeve before I left my condo when I saw a vampire leaning against my driver's door.

"Going somewhere, Amersyn?" Zeke said. He was the vampire I'd stabbed two nights ago and hadn't seemed very happy with me when I'd shown up at their nest.

"How's the shoulder?" I asked instead of answering him.

He grinned, showing off perfectly straight teeth that stood out against his dark skin. "Just fine, thanks to my vampire healing, but you'd know all about that, wouldn't you?"

Smartass bloodsucker.

"What do you want?" I had no qualms about stabbing him again if he tried to get in my way.

He leaned forward, glanced around, and fake whispered, "Didn't you hear? Vampires are real."

My arms crossed. I didn't have time for games. I wanted my bacon fix. "Move, Zeke."

"No can do, hunter lady."

I took a step closer, narrowing my eyes at him. "Why is that?"

"Boss's orders. Someone has to watch your back at all times. We heard some news, and if your protector is unavailable to do his job, he has back-up plan after back-up plan to make sure someone else is. If you have a problem with that, don't take it out on me. My face is too pretty for that."

I couldn't stop myself from laughing and groaning at the same time. Why did these vampires have to seem so normal? I wasn't sure how I was going to get around having them appear all the damn time, but at least they were somewhat tolerable.

I was tempted to stab him anyway and get my brunch, but I was tired. The more I fought them, the more reason they had to be up my ass where they didn't belong.

"I'm going to get breakfast. You can silently get in the back seat or run alongside the car. I don't really care. I just want food."

He chuckled, then opened my back door. "Rachel is going to be so pissed."

I didn't care why, so I wasn't going to ask. These

people weren't my friends. They were vampires who happened to not kill people. Or at least, it seemed that way. I wouldn't ask why Rachel might be mad. Absolutely not.

I got in my car and pressed the ignition. French toast and bacon. That was all I needed to focus on until I figured out a way to strike a bargain with these vampires that didn't have them around me all the damn time.

As I headed out of the garage, Zeke popped his head between the front seats. "Can I turn the radio on?"

"Don't touch my stuff," I muttered. French toast and bacon. French toast and bacon.

"You know, a few months ago, I helped save the supernatural world—possibly even the human one—when we teamed up with wolves and witches. It was pretty badass," he said randomly.

"Why would I care about knowing that?" I asked.

"Because maybe you'd stop inching your hand closer to the knife sticking out of your boot. I can forgive you for stabbing me once, but twice? We're going to have problems."

French toast and bacon. The restaurant was only two more blocks away, but I wasn't sure I was going to make it that far.

"How are you in the sun?" I asked, hoping he hated it enough to stay in the car while I ate in peace.

"My favorite time of the day," he said, then reached into his jacket pocket and pulled out a contact lens case.

"What are those for?" I asked, hoping they were exactly what they looked like.

He began putting a contact in as he answered. "We can't have the humans freaking out. Not all of us are like Maciah who can force his eyes to go darker when the need arises."

With both contacts in, he turned toward me. His eyes were a dark brown. Nothing out of the ordinary. Good for them for thinking outside of the box.

I parked and got out of my Lexus without waiting for Zeke, but he was at my side before I opened the restaurant door anyway.

There was a sign up stating we could seat ourselves. I found a table on the back wall and took the seat facing the door. I was never comfortable not seeing who was coming and going.

Zeke tried to sit next to me until I snarled at him. "Damn, girl. Are you part shifter, too? You know, I have this friend Sam. You'd like her. She hates people, too."

I didn't reply. I didn't want to be friends with his friends.

"What can I get you two?" an older woman asked. She was short, wrinkled, and swayed a little as she stood waiting for us to respond.

"French toast and a plate of bacon," I said.

Her brow furrowed. "A plate of bacon?"

"Yes, a plate," I replied slowly.

She sighed, scribbling on her little notepad. "And for you?" she asked Zeke.

"I'll just eat some of her bacon. You know, since she

ordered a *plate*." He winked at the senior citizen, and she chuckled while walking away.

"Touch my bacon and I will stake you right here where we sit," I said.

He folded his hands on the table and leaned closer. "You take food seriously. I like it. I love food, too."

I bet he did. Just not the same kind as me.

"So, my friend Sam? She's a shifter. Her pack is in Texas, but she hunts people like you do, too. Besides being a...you know, the two of you have a lot in common."

Still, I ignored his attempts at conversation. I didn't care about a wolf shifter. I had no business with them. Vampires were all I hunted, and that was enough.

"At our house, we have all kinds of food. It helps the newborns settle in, even though things don't taste the same as they did before. I like to cook sometimes, but don't usually have time for it. Maciah keeps us pretty busy doing things like you do. I'm surprised we've never crossed paths before."

He had a point with his last comment, but Portland was a big city. It was easy to miss people when they weren't stalking you, but I didn't bother to say that.

Zeke stared at me, but I kept my eyes focused past him and on the door. My nails thrummed on the table as I waited for my food, something I needed even more after being around Zeke. My earlier buzz was wearing off, and the butter knife next to my hand was making me think stabby thoughts.

My breath caught in my throat as Maciah walked

into the restaurant. He searched the room, not stopping until his eyes landed on mine. They were darker than normal, almost the same mahogany as my own, making me forget for the briefest of seconds he was a vampire.

For that one second, I allowed myself to see the man behind the fangs. The man whose eyes saw me and softened, whose hair fell from behind his ear from the incoming wind, and who wore a suit like nobody's business.

"Like what you're seeing?" Zeke said with a waggle of his eyebrows.

I'd done a good enough job of ignoring the vampire, and I wasn't stopping then. Not even if I'd been caught staring. It would only validate what Zeke thought, and I wasn't about to do that anytime soon.

Maciah approached our table, unbuttoned his suit coat, and took Zeke's seat. The other vampire was walking out the door before I could say anything.

The server arrived then as well. "Is this plate enough for you?" she asked, sliding my bacon to me.

There were probably thirty pieces piled up, and I nearly drooled. "It's perfect."

She nodded, setting the French toast down and pointing to the three small cups in the middle of the table. "Maple, raspberry, and caramel syrup. Let me know if you're one of those devils who likes ketchup with your bacon and I'll bring you a bottle for your plate."

I chuckled. I liked her. "The maple syrup is perfect. Thank you."

She cast a wary glance at Maciah. "You weren't here before. Do you want food?"

"No, ma'am. I've already eaten." He smiled at her, and the old bitty blushed. At least I wasn't the only one affected by him. That made me feel moderately better.

She slipped away, humming happily, and I grabbed a fork, pointing it at Maciah before taking a bite of my food. "I left my house in a good mood. Zeke nearly ruined it. Say one word before I've finished my bacon and I'll show you what happens when I'm hangry."

Maciah grinned and said nothing.

I drizzled my plate in syrup, then dug in. I wasn't sure how long Maciah's silence would last, and I wanted to at least be full before I listened to what he had to say. I had hoped for more time to figure out what I wanted to bargain with in order to get them to back off, but I was good at winging things, too.

When I was done eating my four pieces of French toast and two-thirds of the bacon, I wiped my mouth with a napkin and looked back up at Maciah, who was still smiling.

"All done now?" he asked.

I reached for another crispy piece of deliciousness. "Not quite."

"I'd love to say we have all day, but we really don't," he said.

I fake frowned. "Does someone not like to be out in the sunshine?" There really wasn't a ton of sun showing through all of the cloud cover, but daylight was still

HEATHER RENEE

rough for most vampires. I had no problem rubbing that in his face.

"The sun has nothing to do with this, Amersyn. I'd thought when I heard you were a hunter with an impressive kill record that you'd be more mature about this whole thing. I don't like to be wrong, but I always admit when I am." He challenged me and I wanted to smack the smug look off his perfect face.

"Oh, I'm sorry I didn't fall right into line when you told me I'm an heir of an original vampire. Does free will not exist in your world? Because it certainly does in mine," I retorted, tossing my bacon back onto the plate, then pointing my finger at him before he could respond. "I am not your property. You can't just insert yourself into my life without my permission. I don't care what protectiveness you feel toward me. I have done fine on my own for the last seven years, and I'll continue to do so."

I shoved out of my seat and headed for the door, then remembered I didn't pay for my meal. *Damn it!* Turning to do so, I saw Maciah pulling money from his own wallet. Served him right for ruining my morning.

When I got outside, I glanced left and right, looking for Zeke, but he was nowhere to be seen. I went to my car and got in only to sense someone behind me.

"You're not welcome in my car anymore, Zeke," I said as I started the car.

"Good thing I'm not Zeke, then," a woman's voice crooned.

Mother-effing shit.

12

SHARP NAILS DUG INTO MY NECK AS I REACHED DOWN FOR a stake.

"Ah, ah, ah, hunter. Move another inch and I'll rip your throat out," she said, squeezing tighter and cutting my skin.

Well, that didn't work for me, because she was either here to kill me or take me to someone who wanted to kill me. Considering all the crap that had been flung my way the last couple of days, I was banking on the latter.

I moved to reach around and grab her wrist. Before I could, the back door flung open and Maciah practically flew into my car, slamming the woman to the other side of my car.

I really wanted to ask him to kill her outside, but I thought he might not find that as appropriate in the moment as I did.

"What nest are you with?" Maciah hissed in her ear as someone outside—likely Zeke—closed the door so humans wouldn't see something they couldn't understand.

She tried to cackle in his face, but the sound was more like a painful gargle as he gripped her throat. "You already know the answer to that question."

If Maciah did, I was surprised, because I didn't think he knew about Viktor being in town. Maybe he was more in the loop than I realized. Lousy protector if so. If I was him, I'd have handcuffed my ward to my side, but I wouldn't be giving him any ideas.

"I'd ask you to pass along a message, but you're not going to live long enough for that." Maciah reached his other hand to me, and I stared at it. "Unless you'd like blood in your car, I could use a stake," he snapped.

Oh, I'd thoroughly pissed him off this time. Yippee.

I handed him the stake without saying anything. Ash, I could vacuum out. Blood would have been rather inconvenient for me.

"We're just going to keep coming. He always gets what he wants. If you let me help, I can—"

Maciah didn't let the vampire finish. As soon as the stake pierced her heart, her body began to shrivel like fruit being dried out.

I turned my head just in time to avoid getting ash in my eyes. I also didn't want to know how bad of a mess I was going to have to clean up later.

Maciah's touch was soft on my shoulder. "Let me see where she hurt you."

I waved him off. "I'm fine."

"You're bleeding." There was tension in his voice that made my own rise.

I was alone in a car with a vampire, and I was bleeding. How stupid could I be?

Maciah's hand tightened around my shoulder as I began to pull away from him. "I won't ever hurt you, Amersyn. No matter how many reckless decisions you make, I will always come to protect you."

He said the words softly like they were meaningful and sweet, but they filled me with nothing good. I saw red the moment he said "reckless."

I swirled around to him, shoving him into the back seat with more force than I'd intended. "You might not agree with my choices, but that doesn't make them reckless. I don't need your protection, so you're released. Just leave me alone."

"That's not how this works. Rachel said you read the book. Did you not understand—"

I cut him off with a snarl. "If you're about to say something else that implies I'm stupid, I will stake you without thinking twice about it."

My door opened, and Rachel's face appeared inches from mine. "Hello, friend. How about we go for a drive?"

She was grinning widely, and Maciah took the opportunity to exit my car before I did indeed kill him. Argh, he was so frustrating.

Rachel closed the door before I could respond and was sitting in the passenger's seat within two seconds.

"Alright, let's go. Anywhere you'd like. I'm yours for the day. We can talk about what an asshole Maciah is the whole time, too."

I grunted and put the car in reverse. This particular vampire was growing on me like mold on cheese. Technically, it wasn't bad, but...

"I'm sorry I wasn't there this morning. Maciah didn't even tell me he was sending Zeke. By the time I found out, it was too late. I told Maciah you wouldn't be happy, but he didn't listen to me. Freaking men. Never listening because their heads are shoved too far up their asses."

Rachel's little rant made me feel the tiniest bit better. If I was going to be stuck working with these vampires, I was glad one of them recognized the idiocies.

"Maciah is supposed to know you best as your protector, but I knew after staying with you last night that he would get it all wrong. I tried to warn him. Well, you see how well that worked. At least he stopped that bitch from ripping your throat out. I was heading toward your car already, but Maciah sped past me, and you know the rest. So, where are we headed?"

I chuckled. "You really love to talk, don't you?"

She covered her mouth and said something that sounded like an apology.

"It's fine. For now. Just not always," I said.

Rachel nodded, glancing out the window as I got onto 84 East. "Where are we headed?"

"The opposite direction of your mansion," I replied.

She clapped her hands. "Sounds good to me."

Just as we got to the final exit of the city, three black SUVs came racing up behind us, blocking in my car. I let out a groan as soon as I saw them, and Rachel was typing on her phone.

"Take the next exit," she demanded, and I listened. We weren't going to lose these assholes on the open road.

She was switching between her messages and maps app while she told me when to turn. One of the SUVs missed the exit, but two of them were still chasing us.

"At least they're not shoo—"

I covered her mouth. "Don't you dare finish that sentence and make it become real."

"Girl, you are so smart. Left, now!"

We turned down an alley, only one SUV behind us now. I sped up, finally recognizing where I was. I spent most of my time on the opposite side of town and was grateful for Rachel's help getting us this far.

I ran a red light like an asshole, thankful there were no other cars going through the opposite green one. We made three more rights and two more lefts before I started to loosen my grip on the steering wheel.

"Do you think we lost them?" Rachel asked, scanning outside the windows.

"I don't know, but we're not going to stop driving until we're sure." Just as I finished my sentence, one of the SUVs slammed into the side of my car and sent my car rolling into the other lane and landing upside down.

"Amersyn!" Rachel yelled.

"I'm fine. We need to get out," I hissed through my teeth, trying to figure out the best way to get out of my seatbelt without further hurting myself and landing roughly on the ground. At least I wasn't an idiot who didn't wear their seatbelt.

I wasn't actually fine, but she didn't need to know that. My vision blurred. I had a gash on my forehead, likely from cracking the window with my head on impact, and my ribs were definitely broken this time.

"No, stay in the car. Help is already here," she said.

Of course, she'd been texting Maciah. I didn't blame her, though. If we'd have gotten away, I might have been more pissed she contacted him, but I was in no condition to fight.

Rachel was already out of her seatbelt and reaching over to help me, so I wasn't left dangling precariously in the air. She wrapped one arm under my shoulders and unbuckled me with the other before gently setting me on the headliner of my precious car that was now a tangled mess.

"Thanks," I said before bending down painfully to stare out the shattered window.

I couldn't see unless I moved in a way that had me wanting to cry out in agony. Apparently, getting in a fight with a group of vampires two days prior and not resting before getting into a car accident meant I'd be spending an extra few days in bed.

Shoes crunched over glass, and I reached for my

boots to get a weapon, but Rachel stopped me. "It's just Maciah and Zeke."

I relaxed, but only a bit. I wasn't in the mood to have Maciah talk down to me again. I understood that he felt he had to do certain things and be a particular way, but I'd been on my own for a long time, doing things the way I wanted. I was trying to come to terms with everything being thrown at me, but I wasn't perfect, and I needed more time. If we were going to work together, he needed to understand that and respect it.

Maciah ripped my car door off its hinges, and I pouted. My poor, poor car. He leaned in, eyes red with rage, and reached for me without saying a word.

I considered telling him I could walk, but something told me I was better off keeping my mouth shut. I knew how to cooperate when absolutely necessary.

Rachel and Zeke were right behind us. She gave me a thumbs up as Maciah led us toward a silver Mercedes. He got into the back, with me still in his arms, while Rachel and Zeke got up front.

Nobody said anything as Zeke drove us toward their mansion. At least, that was where I assumed we were headed.

Maciah's hold on me never loosened, and he didn't once look at me. Instead, he glowered out the window as I stared at his sculpted face, waiting for him to say anything. Even if he was going to be a jerk.

As the car pulled into the private property, I sighed. Okay, maybe I'd overreacted a little and deserved a little of Maciah's wrath, but I was doing my best.

Accepting that not everything was as I believed wasn't something that could be done overnight and that was what they seemed to expect from me.

Maybe not Rachel. I actually did like her. She could be my friend, but Maciah needed to cool his balls off for a minute.

Maciah carried me into the house, and I expected us to all head to his office to talk, but at the top of the stairs, he turned toward his vampires. "I want a crew watching the fence line every minute of every day. If someone gets onto our property who doesn't belong, I will kill every vampire that wasn't where they were supposed to be."

Geez, that was a little excessive. I opened my mouth to say so, but Maciah snarled at me, and I shut my lips. I could have that argument with him later. It wasn't like I was going to be there forever, so they probably didn't have to worry about psychos trying to break in for long.

"I'm taking Amersyn to my room to talk. Do not disturb us unless it is absolutely necessary," he finished and turned around before either Rachel or Zeke responded.

I tried to speak up. "Do I get—"

"No," he snapped before I could finish.

"But what if I—"

He snarled again, lowering his voice. "I said no, Amersyn."

Okay, I must have bumped my head harder than I realized, because that was hot as hell. Instead of continuing to piss him off, I twirled my thumbs as we travelled down a hallway I hadn't seen during my last visit.

The house was probably over ten thousand square feet. I thought about asking for a tour but figured Rachel would be better for that. Yeah, I'd ask her.

Just as soon as the beast released me.

13

MACIAH MARCHED US INTO A MASTER SUITE FIT FOR A king. Two oversized white doors were shoved open to reveal a bed bigger than any I'd ever seen. It was covered in black silk sheets and minimal pillows.

There was a balcony to the right and only one other window. A small desk was pushed against one of the walls with papers and books stacked on top. A few paintings graced the cream walls. Dark images of forests and castles and stormy nights. Exactly what I expected from the alpha vampire.

He pulled one of the sheets back and lay me on his bed. I sucked in a breath as my ribs yelled at me. Mother eff, I was in pain.

Maciah brushed my hair back. "What can I do?"

"Nothing. I just need to go home and rest for a few days. Something I should have done after the fight the other night, but I had vampires showing up at my condo that put me on edge." Blaming him wasn't fair, but I couldn't help the snark in my words when he had me feeling things I didn't want to.

"You can't go home, Amersyn," he said.

I tried to laugh, but it was more of a groan. "Yes, I can."

"Do you not understand who is hunting you? This isn't a game. This isn't someone you can fight on your own."

I tried sitting up. I didn't like him leaning over me, making me feel small, but damn, my body was well and truly pissed off at me.

"I know exactly who is after me. Viktor doesn't scare me," I said confidently.

Maciah's lips thinned, and his eyes narrowed. "Viktor who?"

"I don't know his last name, but you said you know of the crew who attacked my family. I don't think I killed that Viktor like I hoped."

Maciah was on his feet and pacing before I could blink. He went to his desk, shoveling papers around.

"Why does that seem to stress you out? I thought you said only Rigo and Dmitri were an issue?" I knew why *I* was pissed off that Viktor was alive, but I didn't think Maciah would care. He'd told me the other three vampires were throwaways, easy targets, basically making me feel like I hadn't done anything grand when I'd killed them, or assumed I did.

He looked up at me with dark eyes. "So did I."

"What's that supposed to mean?" I asked, moving agonizingly slow out of the bed.

"It means that you are not allowed out of my sight. You have two vampires after you—two very powerful ones—and one of them has been setting you up since the moment you thought you killed him." Maciah was flipping through another old book as he spoke. I was barely halfway to him when he smacked one of the pages and muttered unkind words.

He strode toward me, holding up the book and pointing to a portrait. "Is this the Viktor you killed, or thought you did?"

The image was greyscale and on yellowing paper, but I'd never forget that face. With a significant widow's peak and beady eyes, Viktor was the easiest of them to recognize. The one I watched kill my mother.

"That's him," I said.

"That's not good, Amersyn. I was told wrong information. This wasn't the Viktor that took credit for killing your family and the one I know *is* dead. You must have gotten lucky stumbling upon this one when you did. When you fought him, did he know who you were?"

I thought back to that night, trying to ignore his "lucky" comment. I'd been hunting. Luck had nothing to do with my kills.

"He should have known. I might have mentioned my family as I drove a stake through his chest," I said, realizing that was a mistake I shouldn't have made, but I was a new hunter then.

Maciah was standing before me within a blink of an eye. He grabbed my shoulders gently, lowering himself until our eyes were level. "Amersyn, I need you to take this seriously, and I need you to forgive me."

"For what?" I asked hesitantly. If he thought he was going to lock me up, he had another thing coming to him.

He guided me back to the bed, and I was silently thankful, even though I was wary about whatever he had to say. I could feel my healing kicking in, but it wasn't quick enough.

Maciah sat next to me, keeping a distance between us. "I asked you to help me kill Silas, not only because I want him dead and I can't kill him myself, but because as soon as I knew who you were, I also knew it was only time before others did. Your vampire traits are growing stronger, and there is one thing Silas has always wanted: an original's blood. I thought if we could kill him before he found out you existed that everything would be fine, but that didn't happen. Somehow, he knows who you are. That's why I sent Zeke to watch over you this morning. He's going to come for your blood."

"I'm sorry, what did you just say? Another vampire is hunting me, and you thought I didn't need to know before anyone else? Instead, you sent a babysitter after me?" I was seething. I wanted to strangle him. He was supposed to be my protector, but keeping me uninformed wasn't the best way to keep me safe.

He began to speak, and I held my hands up, moving off the bed and making my way toward the door. I ignored the searing pain in my sides and the lightheaded feeling rolling through me as I struggled to walk. A part of me knew I should stay, but how was I supposed to trust this nest if they didn't tell me the whole truth?

"I can't do this, Maciah." I reached for the door, barely cracking it open before he was standing in my way.

"You're not leaving this house, Amersyn," he nearly growled.

"Fang you, dude. Get out of my way." As the words left my mouth, I wanted to bury myself six feet under. My brain had officially turned on me. Apparently, I was still my mother's daughter. She'd never liked bad language. I tried to honor her by sticking with the least foul. Usually that worked just fine. Until my emotions were all over the place and I wanted to cry from the broken bones inside me. Then, I spat out stupid crap like *fang you*.

Maciah could barely keep a straight face as I glared at him, trying not to show my embarrassment. "Make me move, Amersyn. If you can do that, I'll let you leave."

I badly wanted to punch him or stake him or anything that would cause physical harm, but I didn't have it in me. My conscience was creeping in as he stared at me with his not-quite-vampire eyes.

A heavy sigh left me as I turned back toward his bed. I wanted to be stubborn and fight him. I wanted to show him that I didn't need their help, but I couldn't. The more twisted this situation became, the more I realized I was going to have to make some major concessions. Plus, I needed sleep more than I needed to escape.

I'd been through enough hell in my life that I knew I was acting emotional. I was hurting from the car accident. My head was a mess from all these revelations, and a good night's sleep was the smarter choice. I'd said my piece and hoped he heard me. Tomorrow, we'd sort out the rest of the details.

"Fine, you win for today, but this isn't permanent," I muttered, crawling back into the bed. Slowly.

The bed dipped, and I cracked an eye open to find Maciah leaning over me. "This isn't about winning against you, Amersyn. It's about keeping you safe. I'm not trying to control you. I'm trying to keep you alive."

I nodded, closing my eyes again. He was probably telling the truth, and I probably needed to accept that, but first, sleep. Later, I'd worry about two psycho vampires and my newly assigned protector and what that all meant for me moving forward.

WHEN I WOKE UP, THE SKY WAS DARK AND THERE WASN'T a clock to be seen in the room. I took a deep inhale, and the first thing that hit me was Maciah's citrus scent. Delicious bastard. Okay, so maybe my nap hadn't made me any less sour about my situation, but I wasn't going to try to leave, either.

There was a vampire in the room with me, but I

wasn't worried about that. I had a feeling I knew exactly who it was.

"Hello, Rachel," I said.

She clapped, something she did often. "Oh, good! I thought you'd never wake up." A lamp clicked on from across the room, and she made her way to the bed. "How are you feeling?"

I sat up, still sore, but the aches were more manageable. "As long as there are no car accidents on the agenda tonight, I'll be okay."

"Fang no, there aren't," she said, covering her mouth before she burst into hysterics.

I snarled. "He told you?"

Rachel turned sheepish and shook her head. "Did you think I was going to leave you up here alone? I was waiting outside the door and heard you after it cracked open. I almost came in, but you didn't seem to be in real danger."

No, I probably hadn't been, and she might have been in deep shit if she'd come into Maciah's room uninvited.

"Thanks for trying to look out, but let's not repeat that word ever again. At least not in that context," I said.

Rachel grinned, showing off her pointed teeth. "Yeah, that's not going to be possible. I've already used it like three times with the other vampires. 'Fang you' is spreading like wildfire, girl. Don't worry, I gave you full credit for its creation."

I pulled the pillow over my head. "Not really necessary."

"Fang yes, it was." She laughed so hard, the bed shook.

"You can go away now," I said.

She quieted and pulled the pillow away. "Are you actually staying? I know Maciah can seem overbearing, but he really does mean well. He's one of the good ones or I wouldn't be here."

I already knew she was right. I just didn't enjoy admitting it. While my nap hadn't made me any less sour about my situation, the rest had given me time to calm down and think with a clearer head. I might not be thrilled about what I needed to do, but I wasn't going to be stubborn about it.

"Yeah, I'm staying. For now. So long as he's not withholding any more secrets from me," I said.

Rachel let out a low whistle. "Speaking of, you must be the most unlucky hunter and vampire heir ever. Silas and Viktor are no joke. I've only been around Silas a handful of times and never met Viktor, but I've heard plenty of stories about both." She shuddered, and I tried not to let her words add to my stress.

"Right. Well, soon they'll both be dead," I said, and I truly believed it. I just needed to get healed and… "Where are my things?" I asked her. I needed my crossbow. If that was gone, I didn't know what I would do. It was the last thing I had of my father's. The father who raised me anyway. My life had become a soap opera, and I wasn't thrilled about it.

"Don't worry. Zeke and I went back to your car and condo. I packed up as much as I could, including your hunting stuff. Though, Maciah said that bag needed to stay in his office. He doesn't seem to think you won't kill him given the first chance."

Ha. At least he was properly afraid of my skills. That made me feel better. I had no intention to kill him anymore, or any of the vampires that lived in this nest, as long as they didn't give me a reason. I had enough to worry about and knew when to choose my battles. Sometimes, it just took me a hot minute to realize certain things.

I was the daughter of an original vampire.

One day, I would become the very thing I hated most in the world.

There was also a chance I was attracted to a vampire.

None of these things had been part of my plan, but if there was one thing I was good at, it was winging it. I'd roll with these punches and come out stronger than ever, because that's what I did best, even when I wished I didn't.

I survived.

14

THREE DAYS HAD PASSED SINCE THE CAR ACCIDENT. THREE days, I'd been trapped in a vampire nest with people I didn't want to like, but they were making it hard for me to keep my resolve.

Rachel never left my side after I'd been given my own room. Apparently, she was training to be a nurse in her former life and was enjoying being able to put those skills to use. Though I was healing just fine and didn't really need assistance, I'd let her stay by my bedside because it was better than the alternative.

Maciah West. Vampire leader. My protector. A whole lot of man sat behind those fangs, and I wasn't sure what to do about him.

The book said relationships between heirs and protectors weren't romantic, but that was likely only because there was a breeder waiting out there somewhere for the heir. I wasn't going to have a breeder. At least, I didn't think so. Shit, was I expected to pop out original heir vampire babies? That was going to be a hard pass for me.

Images of dark-haired toddlers with mahogany eyes flashed through my mind, and I had to shake my head to clear the thoughts. I needed to get out of this house.

"Hey, Rach?" I called. She was in the bathroom, but back at my side within a second.

"Everything okay? Do you need anything?" she asked with a smile, always so helpful and happy.

It was literally impossible to hate her. I'd tried hard enough to realize that.

"I want to go to my apartment today. I'm completely healed and need some fresh air," I said.

She frowned. "We'll have to ask Maciah."

"He might be your boss or whatever, but he isn't mine. I didn't think I was a prisoner here." I sat up in bed and reached for my phone. Maciah hadn't been around this morning, and I knew the stalker had already put his number in my contacts.

I called him, but it rang twice then went to voicemail. Some protector he was. I resorted to texting.

Me: I'm going to my apartment. I'll be back later. Don't make a big deal about it.

Maciah: I'll be home in twenty. Don't leave until then.

Me: Don't be late or I'm leaving without you.

That was just enough time for me to shower and be dressed. If he was even a second late, I wasn't waiting around for him. It was already hard enough for me to be on Team Vampire.

"We're leaving in less than twenty minutes," I told Rachel on my way to the bathroom.

"Does Maciah know that?" she asked hesitantly.

"He sure does."

She shook her head. "You're going to get me in trouble, and I'm going to have to live with you. Just remember that when I go along with your plans."

I laughed as I closed the door behind me. The idea wasn't terrible. Rachel was good people, even if she drank blood for breakfast, lunch, and dinner.

I showered and dressed quicker than normal. We were waiting in the garage, and there were only two minutes left to Maciah's deadline. Every second that passed had my foot tapping faster. Rachel had her own vehicle, and we'd be taking that if Maciah wasn't there soon.

"Let's wait in the car," I said to Rachel, nodding toward her white Audi coupe.

"Are you sure?" she asked as she unlocked the car.

"Absolutely." I slid into the passenger seat just as the garage door next to us opened. "Damn," I muttered as I got back out of the car, staring over the hood at Maciah's silver Mercedes.

He rolled down the tinted window. "Get in."

My stomach rolled at the deep tone in his voice and glower of his dark eyes. I clenched my hands, trying to regain my composure. Maciah would be able to sense my increased heart rate if I didn't control my hormones.

I'd considered being one of those girls that thought if she just gave in once to her wants that they'd be satisfied and I could get over whatever attraction was stirring between us, but I wasn't dumb. I'd already had a taste of Maciah. Anything more would ruin me. No matter how much I hated what he'd been forced to become, I knew if I let him in, there would be no letting go.

I wasn't sure if I could subconsciously ever be okay with that. It wouldn't be fair to Maciah to let him in and hate him at the same time. Seven years of feeling one way wasn't going to be easy to break, but I was slowly coming around to the idea that maybe things could be different. Just maybe.

Rachel got into the back seat of the Mercedes before I'd even closed the door to her car. I made my way to the passenger seat and sat as close to the door as I could. I didn't want the citrus scent coming from Maciah to mess with my head. I needed to be focused.

There were still vampires looking for me, and this was my first time out since they'd found me and totaled my car. Nobody knew how they'd found me, either, which wasn't good.

I had stakes in my jacket as usual and new daggers, courtesy of Rachel, tucked into my boots. While I didn't enjoy the snow falling on the ground, being able to wear extra layers and hide my weapons was always a plus in the winter.

"What do you need from your apartment?" Maciah asked, breaking the awkward silence.

"Uh, my condo. Like, the whole thing. It's my home."

He scoffed. "That's not your home. You barely stay there."

"Yeah, well, it's my personal space and I'm all healed up now, so I can defend myself. I don't need to stay locked up like a princess in your castle." I wasn't sure why Maciah thought I would willingly stay with him for an extended period of time. Even if I was accepting them, I had been living on my own for a long time. I didn't plan on changing that.

Maciah said nothing more as we drove to my condo. When we pulled into the garage, I handed him my key and he chuckled at my card before swiping it across the screen.

"What?" I asked.

"Ms. Smith. Super original and doesn't at all seem suspicious," he replied, sarcastically.

I snatched my card from him once he was done scanning it and gave him a hard shove. "You're a prick."

"So you've said," he deadpanned, driving into the garage.

It was a sad sight to see my empty parking spot, knowing my poor car had been totaled. Insurance was going to pay me out on it, but what they thought it was worth was nothing compared to my value on the car. I'd get another, but it wouldn't be the same.

Maciah parked nearest to the elevator, and we all got out together. Rachel looped her arm through mine, and we walked ahead of Maciah. "You know, if you wanted to live here and Maciah didn't want you alone, I could stay here with you as back-up."

And that was why I liked Rachel. She didn't say protection, she'd said back-up. Rachel trusted I was capable and saw me as an equal. Not someone to be guarded and protected and kept hidden.

We were all enclosed in the elevator, so I didn't respond to Rachel, but I offered a smile and nodded in agreement to her idea. Maciah merely glowered at the wall.

The ding sounded before the doors opened. When they did, I wanted to scream. I'd had hopes of coming to my condo, confirming everything was as it should have been, and then convincing Maciah to leave me there. All of that was dashed away when I took in the trashed rooms.

Someone had gotten into my condo *again*. This time, they hadn't been there for a friendly visit. My couches were cut apart and tossed on their sides. My windows were cracked from items being thrown at them. My kitchen drawers were lying broken on the floor and the cabinet doors torn from the hinges.

Rachel lay a hand on my shoulder as she followed my silent footsteps toward my bedroom. I pushed open the door and found everything in the main bedroom exactly as I'd left it, except my bed was covered in blood splatter and there was a message written in crimson on the headboard.

You can't run forever. We will find you.

Maciah appeared at my other side. "The rest of the

house is clear. We can't stay here, Amersyn." His voice was kind, but I ignored him, moving to my closet. There wasn't anything in there I couldn't replace. When Rachel had grabbed my things, she used the only bag I had, which already had the few things from my old life I cared about, but still, I wanted to see.

My clothes were still hanging up, but blood had also been splattered in here. I shuddered, wondering where the blood had come from and trying not to think too hard about it.

"Come on, Am. We need to go," Rachel said softly.

I turned around and saw Maciah waiting at the door. His jaw was tight and eyes narrowed. I wasn't sure why he was pissed off. It wasn't his stuff that had been ruined. I was in a state of shock that whoever was after me had found this place so easily. I'd gone to great lengths to keep this one a secret. Clearly, it hadn't been enough.

Mindlessly, I walked to the elevator, but by the time we got back to the garage, my temper had risen, and I wanted to stab someone. So badly that my hands shook as I opened the car door.

"We need to go by the gym where I stayed before," I said to Maciah.

"Why?"

"Because if they found this house, then they probably found the other. Pete is a good guy. If he got hurt because of me...I just need to know." I wasn't sure what I would do if vampires attacked the gym. I did what I did to save humans, not put them in further danger.

I gave Maciah the name of the gym, and he headed in the right direction. I stared out the window, watching all of the roads and the cars we passed. Everything was suspicious to me, and I hated that.

Traffic was crap, and it took us nearly thirty minutes to get there. As soon as I saw the gym, or what was left of it, I punched the dashboard.

"Damn it!" I got out of the car, needing to see if anyone was around who could tell me what happened. The place had been torched, but maybe it happened in the middle of the night when nobody was around. Maybe Pete was okay.

I crossed the street, uncaring when I walked out in front of a car whose driver flipped me off as he passed. The windows were boarded up and char marks scorched the siding.

"There's no police tape," Rachel said.

"So?" I wasn't sure what she was getting at.

"If anyone had been killed, the police would have been here, marking the place off with yellow tape," she added.

Relief filled me, and I nearly cried. I wasn't sure I could stomach the guilt of Pete being dead because of me. Rachel might not have been right, but what she'd said made sense. I was going with that until I was told otherwise.

"How long did you stay here?" Maciah asked.

"A couple of years. The longest I'd been in one place

since I became a hunter. Pete was a good guy. I only left because—" I stopped midsentence. How could I have been so dumb? I'd already known someone knew where I lived. It was why I'd left. But between the attack from the other vampires and then meeting Maciah, I'd allowed myself to forget.

"Because why, Amersyn?" Maciah was standing in front of me, worry filling his voice.

"The night you helped me in the alley. I'd left the gym because someone had been in my place. They've been following me for a while, and I haven't even noticed. How could I have missed the signs?"

I'd considered myself a savvy huntress. I was damn good at what I did, but was my focus so singular that I'd left myself vulnerable? I thought I didn't need the vampires, that I could finish this on my own and take care of myself, but I was beginning to see I was wrong.

"It's not your fault, Amersyn. These vampires are hundreds of years old. They've been at this game a lot longer than you have. I meant it when I said we'd help you get your vengeance. This isn't over because they found where you lived," Maciah said with a conviction I needed to hear.

I met his gaze. He wasn't judging me. He wasn't blaming me. He wasn't reminding me that I'd fought accepting his help. No, he was merely confirming to me that I wasn't alone.

Knowing that and accepting it were two different things, though. When I was first on my own, I had trusted another hunter, one who I thought was my friend and cared about me, but things hadn't worked out. After that, I never thought I'd let anyone else in.

Living that way was no longer an option. The risk of letting these vampires in was less than staying on my own. I could see that now.

"Thank you." I nodded at each of them.

Rachel tossed her arm around me, turning back toward the car. "We have your back. That's what friends are for."

I tried to smile, but I didn't have it in me. Instead, I got back into the car and headed to my new temporary home.

A vampire nest.

15

When we arrived back at the mansion, there was a new Audi in the garage I hadn't noticed before. It was a powder-blue color with chrome trim and wheels, along with a busted front end. Someone had been on an adventure.

Rachel bounced in her seat. "Nikki's home. I'm so excited for the two of you to meet."

After the morning I'd had, I wasn't really in the mood to meet new people, but I didn't think I really had a choice.

Maciah grabbed my hand as Rachel exited the car. "Can we talk?" he asked.

Rachel peered through the front window and continued on when neither of us moved.

"Sure," I replied. Hopefully chatting with Maciah was better than meeting another Rachel. I liked the vampire, but I wasn't sure I could handle two of her.

"Are you okay?" he asked.

"I'm fine."

He sighed. "No, you're not, and that's okay. Your personal space was invaded. Somewhere you thought was safe is no longer. That's a big deal."

Maciah was right, but I wasn't going to tell him that.

"It's really not. I move around a lot. I'm used to finding new places to stay. Though, I never expected a vampire nest would be one," I joked, trying to keep the conversation light.

He squeezed my hand tighter. "You might not think I do, but I know enough about you, Amersyn. Not the little things that matter, but enough for me to tell you're not okay. Up until now, the fight has stayed outside of your personal space. Now, it's invading every aspect. That's a lot to take in."

I turned away from him, staring at the garage wall. Seeing my condo ruined and the gym burned? That was a lot. Accepting the fact that I was better off living with vampires than I was on my own? That was even more.

I wasn't going to fight the changes, but that didn't mean I was okay with them. Somehow, Maciah saw that, and I didn't know how that made me feel.

Confused. Grateful. Annoyed. Intrigued. All of the above.

When I didn't respond, he continued, "You're safe here. I won't let anyone get to you. Not even Silas or Viktor."

"Why? I wanted to kill you." I knew there was some magic juju that bound him into feeling responsible for me, but there was something more there. I wanted to know if he felt it, too.

His other hand cupped my cheek, turning my head until I met his stare again. "Because you're special, Amersyn. Not just because you're an heir, but because of who you are and what you're fighting for. What you do means something. It's not just about the vengeance that you deserve. There is a whole world of humans you're fighting for. Maybe you don't realize that yet, but I do, and I want to be part of that. With you."

I leaned into his hand still on my cheek. Where I expected coolness, all I felt was warmth. Everything about him was different. His smell. His touch. The feelings he evoked within me.

"Why is your scent different from the others?" I asked, not ready to address the deeper things with him.

"Heirs are usually still mortal when they meet their bonded. I don't know for sure, but I assume it's so you feel comfortable around me."

Yeah, that made sense. It would be a bit harder to accept his closeness if he smelled like death all the time.

"What about your eyes? All of the vampires here have more brown than red ones," I said, noticing that his were even darker than normal with only slight tinges of red in them.

"Vampires that drink from blood bags don't get the same effects the others do. We're still just as strong after we eat, but for some reason, we don't get all of the negative side effects," Maciah answered.

I didn't recall ever killing a vampire without red

eyes, which made me feel better. I hadn't murdered someone trying to live a better life.

His thumb stroked under my eye. "Yours have a red tint to them."

He wasn't wrong, but I'd always preferred to call the color mahogany and never really thought much of it until I learned I was going to be a vampire after I died. It was good to know that if things changed and I decided to stay a monster, I wouldn't have blood-red eyes.

"I know you're not ready to talk, but I'm a patient man. We're going to figure out who is doing what and how to stop them. Neither Viktor nor Silas will get their hands on you, Amersyn."

Maciah's words were a promise. One that had my heart opening to him. I didn't think that was good, but I needed to learn to trust him if we were going to work together.

As he held my stare, I considered my options. I could continue fighting him and frustrating myself at the same time. Or I could stop resisting the growing feelings within me and see what happened. The latter hit me in the chest, and I knew I had my answer. I wasn't in the business of denying myself pleasure.

One day soon, I'd get more than the taste I'd already had of Maciah West. I felt that deep in my soul.

He leaned in closer, pressing his forehead to mine. We said nothing as we sat together in the car for several more moments.

"We should probably go inside before Rachel comes searching for me," I said softly.

He grinned. "She really likes you."

"She's not so bad, but don't tell her I said that."

"Your secrets are always safe with me."

Just when I'd thought we'd moved on from the heavy, Maciah's words seared my soul. I was in so much trouble when it came to him.

We got out of the car, and he sped ahead, holding the door to the house open for me. "Show off," I muttered.

"Most girls would call that chivalrous," he joked.

"I'm not most girls." I didn't need doors held for me or flowers or anything of the sort.

He leaned in closer as I entered the house, whispering into my ear, "I know, Amersyn."

I sucked in a breath and paused as his voice did things to me that I never expected. My stomach tightened, and I badly wanted to turn around to press myself against him, getting another taste of the kisses we'd already shared.

His hand pressed against my back. "Rachel and Nikki are waiting for us."

My head shook. Yeah, they sure were.

I moved ahead and, thankfully, Maciah gave me some space. Something told me the sexy vampire was enjoying every moment he made me question my entire existence.

Following the sounds of laughter, I found Rachel in the living room that I hadn't spent any time in yet. Zeke was also there, lounging on a couch, and a woman I assumed to be Nikki was standing next to Rachel.

The new arrival had long white-blonde hair with dark roots, the same eyes as the rest of the vampires here, and tanned skin. She wore skinny jeans with short tan boots and a loose yellow tank top that showed off a cleavage line I was slightly jealous of.

Nikki smiled at me. "You must be Amersyn."

I nodded. "And you must be Nikki."

She brushed her hair back. "That's right."

Well, this was awkward.

Rachel came to my side. "Amersyn is going to help us kill Silas. Isn't that great?"

"It sure is. If he doesn't kill all of us first," Nikki replied.

Zeke yawned from the couch. "He doesn't stand a chance against us."

"If he gets his hands on that one's blood, then he does." Nikki gestured to me, and I didn't like the implication.

"We're not going to let that happen," Maciah said, moving closer to me.

"Well, he's getting closer. That's why I came back early," Nikki replied.

"How do you know?" Maciah demanded. I wasn't sure if that was how he spoke to his vampires in general or if it was just the particular conversation making him moodier.

She eyed me. "Maybe we should take this in your office."

Rachel gasped, and Maciah snarled. They weren't okay with the obvious insult toward me, but I understood. Nikki didn't know me, and she was smart to be leery. I was a hunter in their nest. Me being heir meant nothing, given my history. I appreciated her hesitancy.

"Amersyn is living here now. She is on our side, and there isn't anything we need to keep from her," Maciah said.

Nikki nodded, lowering her head slightly. At least she had respect for her nest leader. "Marcella took me to a club down there. Don't worry, I didn't drink from the tap, but I did hear a few things. Silas has moved his operation from Sacramento to Salem. Not all of it, but a decent portion."

"Did you hear anything about Viktor Cross?" Maciah asked.

She shook her head. "I thought he was dead. Or MIA, at least?"

I scoffed. "Yeah, so did I."

"So, what does that mean for us?" Rachel asked.

"Silas is making his moves sooner than we hoped. He knows that if he can get to Amersyn before she becomes a vampire, he'll stand a better chance at getting what he wants: her blood. We'll need to make sure those living here are aware of the risks while Amersyn is in the house," Nikki said.

Guilt filled me as Nikki made it sound like people would be dying on my behalf. I shouldn't have felt bad at all. That was ridiculous. These were vampires. The me from a week ago wouldn't have cared if they were slaughtered, but after spending nearly a week around them, realizing they were more like humans than most supernaturals I'd met, it was hard to ignore the guilt.

"Amersyn isn't going anywhere if that's what you're getting at. The vampires living here are not prisoners. They'll be notified and will have a choice to stay or leave. We've been wanting to end Silas for years now. This is our chance, and we won't ignore it. Amersyn can kill him, unlike the rest of us," Maciah said.

"Why haven't you sent anyone outside of your nest after him before?" I asked.

Rachel sighed. "We have. Shifters, witches, and vampires. They were either killed or paid a higher price to come back after us or just disappeared. We haven't found anyone with a strong enough reason to follow through until you."

Yeah, I had no problems finishing the task. I could see why my hate of vampires appealed to Maciah so much, even though he was one.

"I have some calls to make. Are you good here?" Maciah asked me.

"Of course."

"I am bound to protect her. Remember that." He looked at Nikki, then turned away.

Zeke followed him out of the room and the silence became painful quickly.

"Well, I'm going to go to my room," I said to Rachel.

She frowned, clearly disappointed this introduction hadn't gone the way she hoped.

I headed for the hallway that would take me to the stairs, but Nikki called out, "Wait."

"Yeah?" I asked.

She sighed. "Come sit with us."

I raised a brow without moving. She didn't get to demand my presence.

"Please," she added, and I glanced at Rachel whose lower lip jutted out.

"Fine." I went back to the living room and took over where Zeke had been laying. My day had been shit. My condo was ruined to the point that I was probably going to let the insurance company cover repairing the damages just so I could sell the place. I couldn't chance going back there and being vulnerable. On top of that, I still worried about Pete. I needed to reach out to him as soon as I got back to my room. All of that meant I didn't have the patience for someone who wasn't happy with me being in their home. And not just someone, but a vampire.

Rachel sat in the chair next to me while Nikki still leaned against the wall. When nobody said anything, I closed my eyes, trying to pretend I was on a beach somewhere.

"So, Amersyn has this awesome crossbow you should check out," Rachel said.

"Yeah, maybe. What else has been happening while I've been gone the last few weeks?" Nikki asked.

Interesting. I'd have expected her to respond with something bitchy.

"Amersyn stabbed Zeke. It was great. We also have

two new recruits. Eddie and Jazz have been taking care of them. Then, besides the stuff with Silas and Viktor, not much," Rachel added.

I opened my eyes to see how she took the comment about me stabbing Zeke. I hadn't known who he was then, but I also didn't feel too bad about it. He should have known better than to get close to a hunter.

"How did Zeke take that?" Nikki asked me.

I shrugged. "He seemed more shocked than anything. In my defense, I'd never met him before that moment."

"Yeah, don't feel bad about it," she replied.

I chuckled. "I don't."

Nikki smiled for the first time. "Sorry about earlier. I know you didn't ask for any of this. None of us did. All I want is to live this life as peacefully as I can."

"And me being here messes that up," I stated.

"Or maybe it will be exactly what we need to have true peace."

Rachel grinned back and forth between us. "We're going to have so much fun together!"

"Does she ever turn off?" I joked.

"Not that I've ever seen," Nikki replied.

Rachel threw couch pillows at both of us. "Don't be rude."

"Aw, Rach. You know I love your positivity. This house wouldn't survive without it," Nikki said.

"Damn right, it wouldn't. So, what now?"

I glanced at both of them, hoping nothing else. I was

tired and wanted some time alone. I hadn't had much of that lately.

"I need to unpack and get my stuff sorted after being gone. Can we meet up for dinner?" Nikki asked.

"Sounds good to me," I replied, getting up.

Rachel held her hands up. "Wait a second. I just got both of you together and you don't even want to hang out?"

Nikki went to her, giving her a hug. "I missed you, Rach, but I need a minute. We'll have dinner and maybe we can go to Club Nyx later."

"Okay, fine. Am, you want to do anything?" Rachel asked me.

I grimaced. "I'm going up to my room."

Man, how my life had changed. I'd gone from killing vampires to feeling bad about ditching one.

She nodded, thankfully understanding it had been a long morning for me, too.

As I went up the stairs, I tried not to think too hard about this Silas guy wanting my blood and more about all the ways I could kill him.

I needed to up my hunting game.

16

AFTER I'D GONE UPSTAIRS, I TOOK MY TIME GOING through the things I had at the mansion. If I was going to be staying there longer than I'd previously thought, then I was going to get a little more settled.

My hunting bag had made its way into my room. Maciah must have brought it by the night before or after he'd gone off to make his calls. Maybe we were both trusting each other a little more. An odd concept to believe, but it was happening.

I hung up clothes, found spots for various stakes, and put my bathroom stuff where I wanted it. At least if I was going to be stuck here, I had my own en suite. The rest of the room was plain. Nothing other than a bed and a dresser and cream-colored walls. Apparently, vampires didn't decorate guest rooms.

Once I felt a little more settled, I checked my phone. There was still no word from Dave, and I hoped that was a good thing. Then, I wondered if Simon would be horrible enough to turn on his own kind. What if Viktor had asked him to hunt me? Would Simon still take the job? We weren't friends. Not really even acquaintances. More like people who did the same thing and occasionally ran into each other.

I'd find out eventually.

I sent a text to Pete, needing confirmation he was still okay.

Me: Sorry I took off. Something came up. I heard about the gym. Are you good?

Minutes passed, and my unease grew as I stared at the screen. Finally, the grey bubble popped up.

Pete: Yep. I wasn't there when it happened. You have somewhere to stay?

Me: Yeah. Thanks.

Pete didn't reply and I sent nothing else. Maybe I could find him another gym. He might not know the fire was because of me, but I did and that didn't sit right with me.

"Amersyn?" Rachel's voice called from the other side.

"Come on in," I replied, putting my phone on the comforter before sitting up.

She smiled brightly, brushing her long strands to the side as she looked around. "You unpacked."

"Yeah, well, I thought it was a good idea. I'd rather not have wrinkled clothes whenever I leave the house."

She laughed. "Right. Those wrinkled clothes. So, it's

almost dinner time. I was wondering if you wanted to come cook with Nikki and I."

My eyes widened. When they mentioned dinner earlier, I didn't actually think that we'd be eating together. I hadn't seen Rachel eat yet, and my food had been brought to my room when I'd been healing. Half of it had been takeout.

"We try to eat normal food a few times a week. It helps us remember our lives before," Rachel added when I didn't respond.

"Right. Sure. We can do that. What did you have in mind?" I asked, hoping it wasn't raw meat or anything like that.

"We were thinking spaghetti. Simple, but filling. Unless you'd rather something else."

My mind pictured blood sauce and noodles. I couldn't help myself. She must have read the horror on my face when she gave me the option of picking something else.

"No, spaghetti is great. I normally heat up something from the freezer or make a peanut butter and jelly sandwich, so most anything is better than that. As long as it doesn't have onions in it."

"Onions were created by the devil. You won't find them in our food," she replied with a gag.

I got up and joined her. "What about garlic?"

She laughed harder than I expected. "Garlic is a staple for these vampires."

As I closed the door behind me, I realized I didn't

have a single stake or dagger on me. I hesitated and considered going back, but then continued on. These vampires hadn't tried anything on me, and I didn't want to give them a reason to by continuing to arm myself when we were only inside the house.

Rachel took us in a different direction down the hallway. "There are twelve bedrooms and two offices. A dining room we converted into a game area and a media room which gets used the most. Then, the living room and sitting area you've already seen. This is the way to the media room. We have every show and movie ever made available to watch if you can't sleep."

Right. Like I was going to go hang where the vampires went most. Guilt ate at me immediately for the thought. I needed to quit thinking that way if I was going to be staying there for a while.

"How many vampires live here?" I asked

"Around forty. We have others we consider part of our nest, but as they gain control of themselves, they're allowed to leave whenever they'd like. The only ones we keep locked down are the newborns. Maciah doesn't like to clean up messes."

No, I bet he didn't.

"Where does everyone stay if there are only twelve rooms?" I asked.

"The property is a few acres in size. We have small cabins built out in the trees behind the main house where most of them stay. Everyone comes and goes between those and the main house for food and showers and whatever."

That was good to know. I'd have to start paying attention to faces in hopes of remembering them and not accidentally killing them later. Unless, of course, they gave me a reason.

"Here's the media room," Rachel said as she cracked open one side of the double doors.

I peeked in. There were three rows of chairs, a few bean bags, and a popcorn machine I could see before taking in the full wall projection screen. There were a few vampires in there watching a movie I hadn't seen, which didn't surprise me. I'd never really made time for that kind of entertainment.

I closed the door and nodded. "Looks like fun."

"Super convincing, Am. Super."

I just shrugged. I liked what I liked.

We continued, passing closed doors that Rachel said were more bedrooms, then headed to the first floor from the opposite stairs I'd been using. She turned left and we ended up in the kitchen. It was small, like I expected, and I could see the "game room" just on the other side. They had Pac-Man and a Marvel pinball machine plus a pool table and foosball. That was where I might find myself playing if I couldn't sleep.

Nikki was already in the kitchen. She had noodles and premade sauce from a jar already out and a pot of water boiling on the stove. "Who's hungry?" she asked.

My stomach growled in answer, and they both laughed.

"It's weird, right?" Nikki asked.

"Being here, cooking normal food with vampires? No, not at all," I deadpanned.

She grinned. "I was suspicious when Rachel told me about you. I'm sorry again for the way I acted at first, but I think we're going to get along just fine. So long as you don't try to stab me."

"Don't try to drink my blood and I won't," I replied with a wink.

Rachel clapped her hands. "Ahh, this makes me so happy. We're like one big happy family."

Tension tightened in my chest at Rachel's use of family. I'd had one of those before. One of the best there ever could have been. My mom might have kept my heritage from me, but I didn't fault her for that. She'd been left all alone with her secret and done the best she could. The thought of having another family after them was painful.

"So, what do we need to do next?" Rachel asked, reaching for the sauce.

Nikki jerked the jar away from her. "You get to sit there and look pretty. Amersyn and I will handle the cooking. We don't need another cake repeat."

She sighed. "That was not my fault. It was a mistake anyone could have made."

I glanced between them. "What happened to the cake?"

"She used salt instead of sugar. I don't think I've ever tasted anything so nasty." Nikki gagged for emphasis.

Another vampire came in while Nikki put the sauce

in a pot to heat up. He went straight to the fridge, grabbed a bottle of something, then turned to leave.

"Hey, Eddie. How's the newborn?" Rachel asked.

Eddie turned around. He had a black eye, mussed auburn hair, and torn-up clothes. "How do you think it's going?"

I glanced down at the bottle he grabbed. It had a date and blood type on the side. I tried not to be irritated at its sight. Maciah had said all of their "food" was donated by well-compensated humans, but still... I was having a hard time accepting that the bottled stuff was good enough for all of these vampires.

"Let us know if you need help," Nikki said, and Eddie left with a nod.

I stared at the kitchen counter, wondering once again how I had gotten myself into this situation

Rachel approached me, grabbing my elbow. "Are you okay?"

"Yeah, everything is all good." I looked over at Nikki. "What can I do?"

"Grab the bread from the pantry, butter it up, and get it in the oven. I already preheated it."

I turned away from Rachel before she could try to get me to open up. Keeping busy was going to be the only way I'd be able to stay, so that's what I did. I got the bread ready, found a tray, and got the slices in the oven. I'd taken my time, so that when I was finished, Nikki had dishes I could wash.

"You don't have to clean up if you cook," she said.

"I don't mind," I replied, setting a glass bowl in the top rack of the dishwasher.

They let me continue after that, and I finished the dishes only to begin wiping down counters. Nikki grabbed my hand when I was near the stove. "You're freaking me out. Stop."

"Stop what?" I asked, playing dumb.

"Rage cleaning. I used to do that. You know, before. I see now why it used to drive my husband nuts," she said.

"You had a husband?" I asked, sadness lacing my words.

"I did. And a son. They think I'm dead. It's better that way," she replied, voice hard.

I didn't want to pry on a sensitive subject, so I left the conversation alone. I knew how hard talking about the past could be. I was barely able to do it myself without feeling like my heart was going to shatter.

Soon after, our dinner was ready. We got our plates ready and took them to the living room. As we sat down, a group of three guys came in. One of them inhaled deeply, causing me to grip my fork tightly, prepared to use it as a weapon.

"Oh, my favorite. Please tell me there is more," the first one asked.

"Yeah, in the kitchen. Help yourselves," Nikki said.

The new arrivals blurred out of existence before I could blink.

"There really aren't many women around here, are there?" I asked.

Rachel shook her head. "Only a handful, and they're not usually up for socializing after what they've been through."

My heart hurt for them. I hated to think of women being tortured. It made me want to find Silas even sooner.

I took a few bites, because I really was starving, then asked about the bloodsucker. "So, how are we going to find Silas in Salem? You said he's moved, but do you know where exactly?"

Nikki took a drink from a coffee cup, and I tried to think of the liquid as anything other than blood. "No, that's what Maciah would have gone and made calls about. He has other contacts that might help him. I'd imagine he would also reach out to the wolf pack we recently assisted and put them on call in case we need them."

"I didn't think supernaturals normally worked together like that," I said, remembering how Zeke was bragging about saving the world.

"We don't, but Zeke made friends with a wolf named Sam. Her pack was in trouble, and he convinced Maciah to make an exception, even though we knew things with Silas were getting worse again. Though, we didn't know you existed at the time," Nikki answered.

Rachel groaned and put her food down. She acted full, rubbing her stomach, but she'd only eaten a quarter of what was on her plate before reaching for her own mug. "Maciah will have a plan. He always does, and everything will be just fine."

I tried not to laugh as she spoke, settling for just a grin at the way she always held her pinky out as she drank. That girl was the epitome of positivity. At first, I'd thought she would drive me crazy with it, but the more I got to know her, the more endearing I found her personality. There was nothing fake or forced. It was just who she was at the core, and not even becoming a vampire had taken that away from her.

My mind wandered at that thought, and I wondered who I'd have been if my family hadn't been murdered. Would my mom eventually have told me who I was? Did she know that I'd turn into a bloodsucker once I died? So many questions that I'd never get answers to, but I didn't let that bother me.

They were gone, and I wasn't ever going to let anger or disappointment taint the time we'd had together. What was done was done, and there was no going back to change things. All I could do now was hope that I found the remaining three vampires—including Viktor, since he wasn't actually dead—and finish what I vowed to do.

Maciah came down the stairs as I stood to take plates back to the kitchen. Our eyes met, and there was no denying that a connection existed between us. No matter how much I wished it wasn't true.

"If you're all done with dinner, I was hoping you'd come to my office for a moment," Maciah said to me.

I glanced back at Rachel and Nikki. I didn't want to ditch them, but I was also curious what Maciah wanted and what he might have figured out on the calls he'd made.

"We'll catch up later," Rachel said, taking the dishes from me.

I met Maciah on the stairs. His hand settled on my mid-back, and I tried not to react to his closeness. We made our way into his office, and I hurried to one of the chairs, hoping to put some separation between us. Only, that didn't work out at all how I planned.

Maciah grabbed the other chair and positioned it in front of me, then sat. He was close enough that our knees were touching, and if we both leaned forward... I tried not to picture that scenario. Tried and failed.

"So, what's up?" I asked, the pitch in my voice too high to be normal.

"First, I was going to offer to order you food, but I see that's not needed. Second, I wanted to check in on you," he said.

I smirked. "Are you going to do that often out of necessity?"

He leaned forward, reaching for my hand. "Don't act like you have no idea what's going on, Amersyn. There is something more than the need to protect you between us, something that has nothing to do with you being an original heir and everything to do with you being a stunning woman. I thought you would have realized that after our chat in the car."

Well, fang me. There was a difference between assuming the growing connection between us and hearing him come right out and say something. I just hoped that whatever line we were slowly crossing didn't come back to bite us in the ass.

"Nothing to say to that?" he challenged with a raised brow.

I sat up and gestured between us. "Yes, I agree there is something there, but what are we supposed to do about it?"

"This."

17

MACIAH WAS ON HIS FEET, LIFTING ME UP FROM THE CHAIR with his hands tangled in my dark strands before I could think to back away from him. He moved in, only pausing when he was a breath away from my lips. He was giving me the opportunity to stop whatever was happening.

Only that wasn't what I wanted.

I closed the distance between us and grabbed onto his dress shirt, as if it could anchor me to this moment. A moment that was going to change everything. We might have kissed before, but something about this instance was different.

I was attracted to a vampire. In a way, I was bonded to him. I should have run in the opposite direction. Instead, I decided right then that I was tired of being alone.

If Maciah wanted to act on our attraction, then I was game as well. My mouth opened to his, and our tongues danced. I tasted the citrus on him, moaning as he pulled me flush against him. His hands reached down, lifting my legs and wrapping them around his waist.

He walked us backward. I had no idea where he was going. All I knew was that I didn't want him to let go of me. One of my hands still gripped his shirt while the other dove into his longer coffee-colored hair. I tightened my legs around him, feeling his hard length growing between us.

The pressure made me want things from Maciah that I had no business wanting, but still, I couldn't help myself. He was powerful and resourceful. A bit of a prick, but also kind. The fact that he was a vampire didn't bother me as much as it had before. Or at least, that was what I was telling myself.

As our tongues continued to battle, hands roamed over each of our bodies, learning every curve and dip. Maciah had scars I could feel under his white dress shirt that I moved to unbutton, but his hands covered mine as he pulled back.

"Nobody is getting undressed," he murmured against my cheek.

"Why not?" I asked, even though I had no intention of having sex with him. At least, not yet. A man needed to work a whole lot harder before he got all the way in my pants. Protector or not, I had standards.

"Because we have other things to discuss, and if this continues much longer, we won't get anything done," he answered more firmly, and the mood was gone.

I pulled back, supporting myself on his desk as he took two steps away. Yeah, that was probably for the best. Though, I didn't miss the opportunity to let my eyes wander south and check out the growing package I'd been pressed against. Even through his slacks, I already knew he'd be bigger than anyone I'd been with in the past.

Though, it wasn't like I had heaps of experience. There had only been two guys in my life before that I'd gotten serious with, the last being more than three years ago. Yeah, I was overdue.

Maciah adjusted himself when he saw me staring, and I smirked. "Got something to hide?"

"There's no hiding what I have," he replied confidently, moving around me and to the other side of his desk.

I hopped off the wooden surface and watched as he grabbed his phone, checking text messages. "What did you learn?" I asked.

"Viktor's crew is the one who trashed your apartment. Silas is still moving his nest to Salem and wasn't involved. As far as I'm aware of, the two don't know they're both after you. Likely for different reasons," Maciah answered.

"And what reasons would those be exactly?" I knew Silas wanted my blood, and I knew Viktor was likely pissed I almost killed him, but there had to be more to it.

"Silas is an old vampire. He might not look like it, but he's dying. Made vampires aren't meant to live forever. Centuries? Yes, but not for all time. Not unless they're an original."

My eyes widened, and I spoke up. "Does that mean...?"

"That I'm not sure about. Heirs have long been hunted and killed. Other made vampires were jealous of them and that was where things began to go wrong for our kind. When people began to think of us as Night Demons instead of supernaturals. We used to have families like the shifters. Homes like the witches. Now, we do our best to survive."

I glanced around, gesturing to the mansion we were standing in. "Seems like you've done pretty well at surviving."

"You have no idea what I've gone through to make this life, Amersyn." His voice was solemn, and I felt slightly bad for my comment.

He continued. "Back to Silas. Last I heard, he was dying. Sooner than he was okay with. He has been researching since I've known him on ways to become as powerful as an original. Every attempt has failed for him and caused him to become sick. Likely from the dark magic used during his various attempts."

"So, he thinks with my blood that he can be healed and become something he was never meant to be?" I asked.

Maciah nodded. "That is my understanding. I believe he's known you existed for some time now, and the closer he got to you, the closer I was drawn to you. I've lived in Portland for nearly a decade now. We have always stayed out of the shadows where most vampires prefer to live. Until a few weeks ago when I decided it was time we checked in on the other vampires around us."

I'd only been in Portland a few years. My family had been murdered in Eugene, a couple hours South. I'd begun my hunting there, hoping to find answers closer to home, but every move I made brought me further North. I'd thought that was just the direction the vampires were moving, and I had intended to continue on to Seattle soon, but maybe I'd been drawn to Maciah as well.

"When you say he needs my blood, are we talking like just a vial or the whole shebang?" I asked, because that was probably something good to know ahead of time.

Maciah's eyes darkened to almost black. "I'm not sure, but that doesn't matter. We're going to kill him before he gets the chance to take anything from you."

I liked that idea. It was one I could get behind. But one thing I'd learned since officially becoming a hunter was that plans didn't often go the way we wanted. We needed to be prepared for scenarios A, B, and C. If we had to get to D, we were probably screwed anyway, so I never thought that far. Just my opinion. Thankfully, it hadn't been proven yet.

"How do we find Silas?" I asked.

"He's holed up in Sacramento until things are ready in Salem, which sounds like only a few days from now. We've gone to his current nest several times, and unfortunately, he normally has more than enough guards to give us trouble. Silas might be dying, but he hasn't stopped turning new vampires. He is recruiting dozens every month. Some don't survive, or we get lucky and grab them, but most he keeps. There are probably two hundred vampires that live on his property, and from the sounds of it, more than one hundred are already in Salem."

Two hundred... I had a hard time processing that number. I'd been to some big nests, but never had I heard of anything that large. My skin crawled, and my hands itched to go get my crossbow and begin hunting. The best part about my crossbow was I could take out plenty of bloodsuckers from a distance, leaving them none the wiser as to where I stayed in the shadows.

"What about Viktor? Is he only after me because I almost killed him?" I asked, wanting to make sure I got as much information as I could while we were on the subject.

Maciah grimaced, handing me his phone. It was a photo sent by text message from an unknown number. A wanted poster with a question mark inside the shape of a face and a five-million-dollar reward for the death of an original vampire.

"This applies to heirs. Viktor claimed this reward with a photo of your family after they attacked. Now that rumors have begun to stir that an heir still exists, the person who paid him is asking questions. Viktor is under pressure to either prove you don't exist or turn your dead body in."

Damn, that was a lot of money. A lot of motivation. Not only would Viktor be fighting to keep his life, but also so he didn't have to give back the reward money. He'd probably already spent a lot of it.

"Super. So, one wants an unknown amount of blood from me and the other wants my head on a platter. Sounds like a great time to be me," I said sarcastically.

Maciah came back around his desk and grabbed my arms. "I'm not going to let anything happen to you. For now, Silas is our main problem. Viktor's crew might be closer and poking around, but I'm not worried about them, yet. Not with Viktor still remaining in the shadows and Silas making it known that he's getting closer."

A knock sounded at his door, and I took a step away from Maciah before it opened. Maciah stared down at me, hurt showing on his face. I didn't know why I pulled away. Apparently, a part of me still hadn't completely wrapped my head around the fact that I was living with vampires and diving headfirst into an attraction for one.

Hopefully, Maciah understood that I just needed time to fully adjust.

Zeke poked his head in. "Sorry to interrupt."

"We were just finishing. What's wrong?" Maciah asked.

"One of the newborns we've been working on flew off the handle. We're having a hard time getting him to calm down. If you had some time, we could use your help." Zeke glanced at me. "Maciah is the big bad wolf

185

around here. He always scares people into submission. Well, everyone but you."

I grinned. "I'm not easy to intimidate."

Maciah murmured something I missed, but I didn't call him out on it. Instead, I headed toward the door. "You two have fun with the crazy vampire. I'm going to go to my room for the night."

I nodded at Zeke first, then met Maciah's gaze. His eyes were still dark, and my skin shivered at the intensity of his stare. He could never just look at me. He was always searching deeper for something. I equal parts liked and hated it.

"I'll see you later," Maciah said.

"Yep," I replied in a hurry and backed out into the hallway.

Yeah, I was in so much trouble when it came to that vampire.

I headed toward my room with a smile on my face. I'd been around these people for less than a week, but there was something that felt right in my gut about being where I was. I'd had my rules for a long time and for good reason. I'd once let a man influence my choices, but Maciah wasn't like Caleb.

I hadn't thought of his name in a long time, but the closer I got to the others around me, the more I thought about my past and how more than one instance had changed everything for me.

Caleb was a fellow hunter. He was probably still a hunter, but I'd long ago done my best to forget him. He'd found me when I was living on the streets, hiding from Child Protective Services. He took me in, taught me about vampires and how to kill them. We'd grown close. Too close.

I'd allowed my heart to care for him, because I had nobody else left in the world to care for. He took advantage of that and tried to control me. Never again would I let that happen. Looking back, I should have seen the evil in Caleb's eyes.

Maciah might be a vampire, but he wasn't evil. I'd known that since the first time I saw him. Something inside me kept me from killing him. I was going to trust that part of me and break my rules. As long as I was still on the hunt for those who took my family from me, changing things up seemed like the best move at this point.

As I got to my room, all thoughts of the past were shoved back to where they belonged, and I saw Rachel and Nikki waiting in front of my door.

"What have you been up to?" Nikki asked with a wink.

"Learning about psycho vampires," I replied, pushing them out of the way so I could open my door.

Rachel hummed. "Is that why there are newly formed knots in your hair? All from learning and not from anything more frisky?"

I pointed a finger at each of them. "No."

"No what?" Nikki asked as they followed me into my room.

"Just no." I was not having this conversation with

them when *I* barely knew anything about what was happening between Maciah and me.

"Well, fine. You seem a little uptight still, so nothing good probably happened anyway. We're headed out. You're coming with us," Nikki said, and I laughed.

"Yeah, I'll pass." They were already dressed up, something I hadn't paid too much attention to before, but now that they were talking about going out, there was no way I was shimmying myself into a little black dress like the two of them had.

"Come on. You need to loosen up. It's been a long week, and Club Nyx is safe for us to go to," Rachel said.

Nyx? I'd heard of that place. In order to get in, you had to be a member that was invited. An invite that came with a high price tag. The club didn't let humans in, which meant I never thought to try and gain access.

"They're not going to let me in," I said. Even if my sperm donor was an original vampire, I was still human.

Nikki chuckled. "Oh yes, they will. Maciah practically owns that place. He buys all of us that prove our loyalty a membership. We can get you in."

Interesting. I didn't take Maciah for the clubbing type of person, but the other vampires around? Yeah, I could see that. Another reason that made me want to trust him. He took care of his nest. Most people with money didn't do that. They only used their power to control those under them. Just like Caleb had.

Damn, I thought I'd shoved the thought of him back into a box. I needed to try harder. He was my past, and I wasn't going to let that asshole have anything to do with my future.

"Okay, fine. But if one bloodsucker gets near my neck, I'll stake them without asking questions first. Oh, and I'm not wearing a dress. I'll put on boots and a nicer top, but I don't do dresses," I said with my arms crossed.

Rachel and Nikki shared a smile. "Deal," they said at the same time.

Oh, man. I was going to regret this.

18

BEFORE I HAD TIME TO OVERTHINK THE CHOICES I WAS making, I found myself in Nikki's blue Audi and headed to a club I didn't belong in. A club filled with only supernaturals. If I was accepting Maciah's words as truth, then technically, I was one. Except I needed baby steps. I still considered myself human.

I wore my favorite black boots with three-inch heels and daggers tucked inside each of them. I also donned a flowy, black sequin tank. It was loose enough that I could keep a couple of stakes tucked into my pants without anyone the wiser, so long as they didn't put their hands where they didn't belong.

Rachel and Nikki were overly excited. They had the music volume in the car turned all the way up and were singing at the top of their lungs to some rap song I didn't know the lyrics to. I preferred classic rock, but I could tolerate pretty much anything.

We pulled up in front of the sleek club ten minutes

later. There were valets out front waiting to open our doors and take the keys, along with a red carpet leading to double doors where a bouncer stood.

I exited the car, and the valet at my door did a double take at me. He probably knew I was human and was as confused about my presence as I was.

Nikki and Rachel grabbed each of my arms and led me toward the door. Heading down the red carpet felt like I was walking to my death. I should have said no. I should have gotten into bed and stayed put. Instead, I'd agreed and was going to freeze to death without the jacket I should have also brought if we didn't get inside soon.

Rachel leaned in and whispered, "Quit looking like a hostage. They won't let us bring you in if they think you don't want to be here."

"But I don't."

She shushed me as Nikki approached the bouncer. A badass chick that I was pretty sure was a wolf shifter stood with her arms crossed. She was dressed in black leather pants and a red crop top with dark hair braided down her back.

"Nikki, you know the rules," the bouncer said, glancing at me.

"Oh, come on, CeCe. She might seem human, but I assure you she's not. She's our guest for the night," Nikki replied, and I wanted to punch her. I was pretty sure people shouldn't know I wasn't human.

"If she's not human, what is she?" CeCe asked.

Nikki moved in closer. "Can't say. Maciah's rules. You know we don't like to upset him."

Oh, Nikki was devious. I saw the moment the bouncer heard the underlying threat that wasn't at all real. Maciah would be grateful if CeCe didn't let me in. In fact, he was probably going to be livid we'd left without telling him. Something I hadn't really thought about until then.

CeCe sighed. "Fine, but tonight only. You know the rules. Guests only get a pass once. If you want to bring her again, then she needs a membership."

Nikki kissed her cheek. "You're the best, girl."

"Yeah, yeah. Get out of here."

We passed by the bouncer, and I avoided her stare. As the doors closed, darkness enveloped us, and it took a moment for my eyes to adjust. The walls were covered in a crimson velvet, and the floors were a dark hardwood. Lights were up ahead, leading us toward the bar.

As we turned the corner, a dance floor came into view that was lower than all of the seating areas. Overhead, small drop lights hung down from the ceiling, casting ambient light through the room. Bright enough for me to see where I was walking, but low enough that the shadows offered privacy to those who wanted it.

"Let's get drinks first!" Rachel said, pulling me toward the bar.

That was a good idea. They were going to have a hard time getting me to dance if I wasn't liquored up.

Both of them ordered sugary lemon drops, and I ordered a double of Blanton's, neat, gaining an odd look from the bartender, one who had nothing on Dave.

I turned my back to the bar, looking out across the room to see where the exits were, a habit I'd come by on my various hunting trips. There were bathrooms at the far-left corner and an unmarked door on the right side.

"What do you think? So much better than the dive bar I found you in," Rachel said, and I sneered at her.

"Don't diss my bar," I snapped.

Nikki laughed. "Someone's touchy."

"Crossroads isn't the best, but the ones who work there are good people," I said.

"Then, we'll have to check that one out next time," Nikki replied sincerely.

Rachel didn't seem keen on the idea, but I had a feeling Nikki would love Crossroads.

Our drinks arrived, and I had half of mine gone in one gulp as they led me to a table. It was small, but there was room around us to breathe.

"Drinks, then dancing?" Rachel asked, again holding her pinky out as the drink dangled between her fingers.

"Is the pinky thing a habit you can't break or something to make you feel fancy?" I joked.

She glared at me, but also smiled. "I don't want any shit about how I hold my drinks. I've done it since I was a toddler. Tea parties were my jam. I threw the best ones."

Yeah, I had no doubts about that. I took another

drink from my glass and shivered. "This isn't like the bourbon I'm used to."

"Did we forget to tell you these are supernaturally spiked drinks? Yeah, you'll be drunk within five minutes," Nikki said with an evil grin.

"I hate you," I muttered, then hiccupped. This was so not good. I couldn't remember the last time I had been drunk. Being in control of myself was always a necessity.

I pushed the drink away, but the damage was already done. My vision was beginning to blur as the liquor settled in my gut.

"Ready to dance now?" Rachel asked.

I looked around. There didn't seem to be any threats. Everyone was smiling and having a good time and not paying me any attention. I might as well take advantage of the temporary impairment. I wouldn't be letting it happen again anytime soon.

"Let's go," I said with a smile.

They grabbed on to me and led me down a short set of stairs and onto the dance floor. The song changed to *Pour Some Sugar On Me*, one I knew well and enjoyed. Before I knew it, my hands were in the air, and I was swaying to the music.

Okay, maybe being slightly intoxicated wasn't such a bad thing.

The three of us danced through several songs. The longer I was moving to the beat, the more I let my guard down. The vibe in the club was calming, and I understood then why it was so exclusive. I was going to be finding out how I could get a membership, even though I technically didn't meet the requirements to join.

We drew a crowd, and people joined in to dance with us. Women and men. Bodies touched, but I didn't feel threatened. Instead, I closed my eyes and fell into a groove.

Hands grabbed my hips, moving my body in sync with theirs. I considered stepping to the side, but they weren't doing anything more than dancing with me. My eyes opened to find Rachel and Nikki also dancing with two other guys. Everyone was having a great time.

I couldn't remember the last time I'd enjoyed myself that didn't include killing a vampire. I'd worried for a moment that the other supernaturals here would throw a fit about my presence, but that hadn't been an issue at all.

"I'm going to go grab another round of drinks," Nikki called over the music. I nodded, as did Rachel.

I moved closer to Rachel. The guy at my back stayed with me. I hadn't even turned around to see what he looked like. When I thought to do so, my gaze caught someone familiar and extremely furious.

Maciah was standing at the top of the stairs to the dance floor. He had Nikki in his grasp and was staring daggers at me.

His rage was so palpable that I stood frozen where I was. Rachel turned to see what had my attention and winced. "I didn't think he'd get *that* mad," she said.

Yeah, she also didn't know that I had been making

out with Maciah before leaving his office and having him find me with another dude humping my back probably wasn't helpful to the situation.

I shoved the guy behind me away, only offering him a quick glance. "I'd run if I was you."

He was smart and took my words seriously. The guy behind Rachel did the same. I took a step forward, ready to face Maciah. He didn't own me. It wasn't like I'd left alone and was in danger. I had two of his top vampires with me in a club where fighting was prohibited. The risk was minimal.

He closed the gap between us and picked me up, tossing me over his shoulder. Rachel moved ahead of us and headed for the exit with Nikki.

I slammed my fist into Maciah's back, but he wasn't at all deterred. I considered grabbing one of my stakes from the back of my jeans but decided against it. I wanted to be able to come back to Club Nyx one day.

The whiskey was wearing off, and I stopped fighting against Maciah's grip across my thighs. His Mercedes was parked up front, the valet standing several feet away from it.

Maciah dropped me into the passenger seat, then turned to Nikki. "Get your car and come straight to the house."

She nodded and took the keys from the waiting valet. Rachel glanced between the two vampires, seeming unsure what to do.

Maciah snarled at her, and she went with Nikki. I

was going to be facing the pissed-off vamp on my own. Just how I liked it.

He got into the driver's seat and gripped the steering wheel until it began to bend beneath his fingers.

"We were—"

Maciah cut me off. "Not yet."

"But all I was going to—"

"I said not yet, Amersyn," he snarled.

His tone set me off. I wasn't going to be treated like a child. I wasn't acting like one. I was merely with friends who were capable of fighting in a controlled setting. He could be mad we left, but that was it. Okay, maybe because of the guy dancing behind me, but that had been innocent.

"We were perfectly safe back there. Being bound to protect me doesn't make you the boss of every decision I make. Nyx is an exclusive club with rules. One you support. Excuse me for wanting a moment of normalcy after all the shit that's been happening lately," I said, finally without him trying to interrupt me.

We stopped at a red light, and he stared me down. "A club with rules that were broken tonight the moment they let you in. Had it occurred to you that people like Silas and Viktor don't care about rules? They don't live here. They don't care if they're not welcome back at Nyx after they kill you. Things like that don't matter to vampires like them."

He had a point, but still, nothing had gone wrong, and I said as much.

"You don't get it, Amersyn. I'm not sure you will," he said with a tone that sounded a lot like disappointment.

"What's that supposed to mean?" I snapped.

He pressed the gas, and my head slammed into the back of the seat.

"It means that you're young and I shouldn't expect so much from you."

Oh, that little prick.

My fist struck out, but he caught it in his hand. "You can't hurt me. Try all you want, but I have been at this a lot longer than you. As have Viktor and Silas. Rachel and Nikki should have known better, too."

"You're making a big deal for no reason. Nothing happened," I said as I jerked my hand back.

He turned to me. "And what if it had? Did you think about how that would have made me feel? Or were you only thinking of yourself and your need for 'normalcy'?"

His words struck a little deeper. Maybe it had been a selfish move, but it wasn't a spiteful choice to go out with Rachel and Nikki.

I didn't bother to answer him. He had been right before when he tried to get me to stop talking. We both needed a little time to calm down and think about a better way to handle things. I wouldn't be kept locked away forever. I'd rather die than be a prisoner.

We got back to the house. Nikki pulled in behind us, and Maciah immediately got out of the car. He stood in front of Nikki's and addressed both of them in an eerily calm voice. "You two made a decision you had no right making tonight. You know the rules, and you broke them. I want both of you packed and out of here within the hour. You can take the cars and your personal belongings, but nothing else."

My jaw dropped. I was in legitimate shock. He couldn't kick them out for going to a club. I'd had the choice to say no. This was not their fault.

"Maciah!" I yelled after him, but the slamming of the house door was his only reply. I turned to Rachel and Nikki. "I'm sorry. I'm going to fix this."

Rachel sniffled and wiped her cheeks. "We should have known better. Maciah is right. I just wanted you to feel welcome here and a part of something. Not like you were forced to live with vampires."

Nikki wrapped an arm around her. "It's going to be okay, Rach. We'll figure something out."

"I know it's been trashed, and it's not exactly safe, but you can stay at my condo tonight. Maciah just needs some time to cool off."

He also needed a threat or two from me. I wasn't going to let him kick Rachel and Nikki out of his nest. We could each have the night to calm down, but tomorrow we'd be setting some ground rules for all of us.

19

After giving Rachel and Nikki the card to get into my condo, I went straight to my room and locked the door. I didn't want to yell at Maciah. I knew why he was mad, and he was justified, but not to the extent of kicking out the others. That was unacceptable.

Instead of trying to solve things immediately, I went to sleep. Or at least tried to. Most of the night, I'd stared at the ceiling and walls while I tossed and turned.

I didn't want to fight with Maciah. I wanted us to be able to work together.

When the sun rose, I took the chance that Maciah would already be up. I got dressed in jeans and a green long-sleeve shirt. There was snow coming down outside and vampires apparently didn't mind the cold, because I was freezing once I got out of the warmth of my bed.

Heading to the office, I passed by Zeke. He had his head down and paid me no attention. My mind told me that I didn't care why he was upset—that his problems weren't mine—but my heart had other opinions.

I reached out to him, grabbing his arm before quickly letting go. "What's wrong?" I asked.

"Nikki and Rachel are gone. They were part of what made this nest feel like a home instead of just somewhere to live." Zeke's eyes held a longing in them I could relate to.

I didn't know his past life, but something told me he'd had a family that he hadn't been able to let go of yet.

"They'll be back today. Don't worry," I said.

Zeke eyed me. "How do you figure? Maciah was furious with them for taking you out."

"If he wants me to remain here and not be a prisoner fighting for a way out, then he's going to invite them back this morning. Rachel and Nikki did nothing wrong. We were perfectly safe, and nothing happened," I said.

The vampire smiled brightly. "I wasn't sure about you at first, but I think you just might be the very thing we needed in this house to make it a family."

I wasn't sure what he meant by that, and I didn't really want to know. Instead of continuing the conversation, I nodded and walked toward the office.

The door was cracked, so I pushed it the rest of the way open. Maciah was standing at the window behind his desk, his back toward me. There was tension in his shoulders that were covered by another one of his suits. The only time I'd seen him dressed somewhat casually was when he'd found me in the alley.

"Amersyn," he addressed me without turning around.

"Maciah. We need to have a chat."

I closed the door behind me and took a seat in one of the chairs in front of his desk. He turned slowly toward me. Strands of his dark hair hung in front of his burning eyes, and he kept his hands in his pockets while looking down on me.

"About what?" he asked.

"About how things are going to work here if we're going to hunt these vampires together," I replied.

His head lifted slightly. "Do you think you can come in here and make rules for my nest?"

"No, but I know that I'm not okay with being told what to do, and I do want to find a way to work with you. I understand Silas and Viktor aren't to be perceived lightly. I take their threat toward me seriously, but I also won't hide away, living my life in fear until they're dead. You shouldn't ask that of anyone. What happened last night shouldn't be made into as big of a deal as you've made it."

Maciah stepped closer to his desk, placing his hands on the surface. His eyes darkened. "Do you really understand, Amersyn? Did you think going out to a very public club wouldn't put you in any danger?"

"I thought that spending some time with the vampires I need to learn to trust was a good thing. I expected them to have my back if anything went wrong. They never left me alone, and I didn't take off like you probably would have expected me to. Everything was fine."

He slapped the desk. "But it might not have been. That is what you're not seeing." He was seething, and I could hear the fear in his voice.

"I didn't think you were the kind of man who let other people dictate your life. I'm certainly not. There is risk in everything we do in this life. Every day, we wake up not knowing if it will be our last. Don't ask me to live in fear, because if that's what you expect, then we're done. Right here, right now, I'll walk away."

Our gazes locked. I wouldn't budge from this. I made a choice seven years ago to live this life knowing I might die. I was okay with that risk, and while I took precautions when necessary, I never once stopped living and doing what I wanted.

I leaned back in my chair and crossed my arms. I still didn't want to fight with him. I just needed him to understand where I was coming from, but from the creases forming around his eyes, I wasn't sure he was capable.

The silence around us became heavy. He was waiting for me to break or act out, but that wasn't going to happen.

A knock sounded out the door. "Not now," Maciah snarled without looking away from me.

Footsteps retreated quickly, and we continued our standoff.

"I can do this all day, but you only have until

tonight to agree with me or I'm out of here," I said finally.

His lip lifted in a snarl, and he turned away from me. I might not get exactly what I wanted, but Maciah had broken first. I was going to win this small battle.

"Rachel and Nikki can come back under the condition that the three of you are not allowed to leave this house alone," he said, staring back out the window.

"We aren't alone when we're together," I replied with a grin.

He was in my face before I could blink. His hands braced against the arms of the chair I occupied. "You know what I mean, Amersyn." His voice was low and lethal, which should have caused at least the smallest spike of fear to run through me, but it only made me want to challenge him more.

"I won't be your prisoner," I said.

"I didn't say you couldn't leave. I just said not alone. If the three of you want to go out again, then I will go with you."

"Like a fatherly chaperone?" I joked.

He leaned closer, his breath mixing with my own. "If that's what you need, then that's what I'll be, but I'd rather be the man behind you than some wolf shifter I wanted to murder."

He was referring to the guy I'd been dancing with the night before. I wouldn't lie to myself and say I hadn't pretended it was Maciah behind me more than once.

"Fine. We work together as a team. We go places

together. We end this together," I said, trying to keep my breathing steady and ignore his closeness.

"Together," he agreed softly.

We stayed close for several more seconds, and this time, I was the first to break. Yes, I'd admitted my attraction to him the night before, but we were discussing a business deal and I wasn't about to jump him just when we started to agree.

I moved out of the chair and headed for his window, curious as to what he saw when he stared outside. He chuckled as I walked away, but I didn't care. He could have *that* win. I'd gotten what I wanted.

There was a small courtyard below his office with more rose bushes planted in varying colors of red, white, yellow, and orange. The grass was cut perfectly and bright green, and there was a water feature in the middle with koi fish swimming around.

A couple of small canopies were set up with two or three chairs beneath them. A vampire, or so I assumed, was reading a book in one of them. He looked completely at peace and normal. Not at all what I was used to.

"These people just want safety, and they're willing to fight for it. I plan to do my best to give that to them. Even if it's in the smallest of ways, such as providing a comfortable spot to enjoy a novel," Maciah said from behind me.

He had his rules and made sure the vampires lived by them. He was feared yet respected. I admired that about him. Among many other things.

As I turned back to him, Maciah was closer than I'd realized. Our chests brushed against one another, and his hand cupped my cheek. "I just want you to be safe, Amersyn."

"I know. That's the reason I'm still here," I replied.

He closed the distance between us, his lips brushing against mine softly. "Why don't you call Rachel and tell them to come back?" he whispered.

They were safe enough in my condo. They could wait just a little bit longer.

I kissed Maciah first this time. Our business talk was done, and I had no problem picking up where we'd left off before.

I gripped the front of his suit jacket, pushing the material off his shoulders. "You're always wearing so many layers," I complained.

"Maybe I'll do something about that." His fingers gripped my chin, and his tongue moved over my lips. I opened to him, not having succeeded at getting his jacket off.

He pressed me against the window, reminding me of our fight in my condo. I'd known then I was in trouble. Maciah was too tempting. Too different and patient. He was a man willing to do whatever it took to get what he wanted.

I should have been more cautious with him, but I had bigger battles to fight.

He leaned back, rubbing his thumb over my swollen lips. "I need to go check on the newborn."

"I should call Rachel," I replied, but didn't remove my arms from around his neck.

"Have dinner with me tonight," he said.

I nodded in reply as his tongue swirled over my collarbone, making me unable to speak.

"I'll see you tonight, then," he murmured into my ear.

When I opened my eyes, Maciah was gone. I tried to be irritated over the fact he disappeared so easily, but instead, I grinned and headed back to my room.

I had vampires to call.

20

AFTER I CALLED RACHEL WITH THE GOOD NEWS THAT THEY could come back, I checked my phone for hunter updates. There was an app some of us used for passing along information. I didn't bother with it normally, but given I hadn't been on the streets as much as usual, it was probably good to check.

Scrolling through the feed, I searched for anything about Silas, Viktor, or vampires with black rings around their red eyes. Nothing popped out at me, which was weird. I would have thought there would be something exciting—a group kill at a big nest or stopping a blood party—but there was nothing of the sort. Just mentions of vampire sightings.

Dave was next on my list. When I opened my messages with him, I could see he was already typing something to me. I waited not so patiently for his text to come through.

Dave: I'm at the bar doing inventory and a deep clean. I found something you're going to want to see.

Me: What's that?

A picture came through of a hand drawn portrait of me. Underneath the eerily accurate drawing was a price tag of one-million dollars.

Dave: Do you know what this is about? Does it have to do with the group of vampires I told you about?

Me: I don't know. Thanks for the heads up.

Dave: Amersyn, are you okay?

Me: I am. For now.

Someone had officially put a bounty on my head, and it had nothing to do with the original one that Viktor had claimed. My first thought was to show Maciah and see who he thought it might be, but then I worried that he would renege on the deal we'd only just agreed to.

Crap, I had no idea what to do. Just as I considered going on a walk to clear my head, Rachel and Nikki burst into my room without knocking.

Rachel threw her arms over me, holding on tighter than necessary. "Thank you so much! I was pretty sure he'd let us come back home eventually, but I had no idea how long we'd be on our own. I couldn't sleep last night, so I cleaned your condo and ordered all these things for it, thinking we were going to have to live there. I don't think I've ever been so stressed in my life."

Her words were rapid-fire. I grabbed her shoulders. "Calm down."

She took a deep breath and was nearly in tears. "I'm just so glad we met you."

Nikki gave Rachel a gentle push to the side and hugged me as well. "Girl has no control over herself when she's emotional. We're both grateful for you. We should have known better than to go out last night."

I scoffed as she backed away. "We're not prisoners, and I told Maciah that. We can come and go as we please now, but I did agree to allow him to chaperone under the assumption that if he was busy, he'll probably send Zeke instead."

Rachel's eyes widened. They were hazy, and I wondered if they'd been able to eat since they were kicked out.

"You got Maciah to agree to that?" she gaped.

"It was either that, or I left to go live with you two at my condo and figure things out on our own," I replied, then glanced at Nikki. She had the same glazed-over look in her eyes as well. "Do the two of you need to eat?" I asked.

Nikki sighed. "Badly."

I pointed toward the door. "Get the hell out of my room before I have to stake you for thinking I'm a snack."

They both stared at me, horrified. Then I grinned. "I mean, I really would stake you if you tried to bite me, but I know you're both smarter than that. Seriously, though. Go get some proper breakfast."

"Yeah, you have shitty food in your condo. There wasn't even anything appealing to attempt to eat," Nikki complained before they both headed toward my door.

I shrugged. "I've survived just fine on frozen food."

Rachel laughed. "Survived is one word for it."

They left, and I was once again alone in my room, realizing I had no idea what I was going to do about the information Dave sent me.

Two days had passed, and I hadn't seen Maciah once. He'd texted me from somewhere on his property stating he was still having issues with the newborn that required his complete attention. Rachel and Nikki assured me that was normal with about half of the new vampires.

Apparently, weaning yourself off fresh human blood wasn't an easy task. I hoped I never found out why.

I hadn't heard anything else from Dave and tried to get into a new routine while waiting things out at the mansion. They had a full gym in the basement that I began using to keep myself in shape. The vampires steered clear of me, probably because I practiced with a stake just like I had at Pete's gym when I was alone

When I wasn't working out or hanging with Rachel and Nikki, I found myself drawn to the courtyard I'd seen from Maciah's office. The tables were spread far enough apart that I could relax there without being disturbed. Anyone who came and went was quiet, and I appreciated that.

The sun was out, so I was enjoying the courtyard again. I had nearly started dozing off when I sensed someone standing over me. My instincts had me reaching for the dagger in my boot and jumping up.

The metal was an inch from Maciah's heart as he grinned at me. "Still on guard, I see."

"Pretty sure I'll be this way until my death," I said, sliding the weapon back into my boot.

"As you should be," he said, then reached out to gently grab my arm. "I'm sorry I had to cancel dinner. Has everything been okay around here?"

"Well, I haven't killed anyone," I joked. He didn't find my words funny. "Everything has been fine. All of your vamps are surprisingly well-behaved," I added.

"I would expect nothing less. They know the consequences if they act up," Maciah added confidently.

I raised a brow. "Do you enjoy kicking vampires out of the nest?"

"No, but if there aren't severe consequences what would keep these vampires from continuing to kill humans? They have everything they could want here. In exchange, I ask for very little. If they can't respect that, then they're gone. I won't have one ruin all this for everyone else."

Okay, he had a point there.

"Are you all done with the newborn issue?" I asked,

realizing he wasn't wearing a suit. Instead, he was in dark jeans, a dark grey t-shirt, and black boots.

"Yes, I actually just left there and came to find you first before showering and changing."

I grinned and teased him. "Can't go too long without those fancy suits of yours."

His hand wrapped around my neck and pulled me closer. "I was under the impression you liked my fancy suits, even if they have too many layers."

Maciah's voice was a whisper against my ear, and his lips pressed to my cheek before I could respond to him.

"Let me shower and change, then we will have that dinner I had to cancel," he said, pulling away.

Damn, this vampire was going to ruin me with his sex appeal.

He turned back with a grin on his face. "I'll meet you in my office in five minutes?"

I nodded, wondering how in the world he could shower and change that quickly. Well, if he was late, that would give me time to look around and see what new things I could learn about Maciah West.

By the time I'd grabbed my water and phone from the table, Maciah was nowhere to be seen. I wasn't about dressing up, so I headed straight to his office. I took my time, though, going past the media room and peeking in. I'd yet to watch a movie in there. Something about being in the dark with vampires still wasn't sitting right with me. Maybe one day.

There was a large group watching some racing

movie. An echoing "Ooohhhh" sounded as one of the hotrods crashed into a guardrail. Yeah, not my kind of movie.

I continued past and arrived at Maciah's office to find another vampire exiting the room. My suspicions went up. I hadn't ever seen anyone in his private space without him. Before I could question the vampire, he blurred out of sight, and I ran the rest of the way to the office.

Inside, the smell of Hot Pockets hit me, and I started to laugh. The sound grew as I shook my head. "Ridiculous vampire," I said.

Maciah's hands were on my waist. "I thought I was being funny."

I leaned into his touch. He still smelled of citrus, but there was also a woodsy body wash wafting off of him I didn't miss.

I turned around to take him in. He'd changed into Chino-style grey pants—a step above jeans, but not as fancy as slacks—and a white Henley sweater. I instantly thought of Dave, who liked to wear those, and my gut twisted that I still hadn't told anyone about the bounty attached to me.

"What's wrong?" he asked as soon as my mood changed.

"There's something I should show you," I said and reached for my phone in my back pocket. This was going to ruin whatever night Maciah had planned, but I was pretty sure he'd rather know.

I pulled up the texts from Dave.

"Who is 'My Bartender'?" he asked suspiciously.

I smirked and considered messing with Maciah, but then thought better of it. He'd had a long few days, and I needed to show him the photo before I changed my mind.

"He's my very good-looking and very gay bartender who is in a committed and happy relationship," I replied, then gave him my phone.

He zoomed in on the picture, jaw tightening as he saw it, forgetting all about talks of my hot bartender. "How did he get this?"

"Dave works at Crossroads. He found it while they were doing a deep clean of the bar a couple days ago."

"And he just now sent it to you?" Maciah snapped.

"No, he sent it to me immediately. I'm just now showing you, and before you get mad at me about that, you were busy. I specifically didn't request to leave the house because of that fact. I'm not an idiot," I said, hoping to defuse the bomb within him before it went off.

"You shouldn't be alone at all, Amersyn. What if one of my vampires finds out about this reward? Everyone is a good person until they aren't."

I wanted to remind him that those who lived under his roof weren't actually people anymore. They were vampires, and he was right.

He started poking around on my phone. "What are you doing?" I asked.

"Forwarding this to myself. I see you've changed my name in your phone," he muttered.

Oops. I'd done that when I was mad at him. He was in there as "Stupid Prick Vampire". I liked having nicknames for all of the contacts in my phone. It kept things interesting until said person actually saw the name.

He continued to tap on the screen, then handed me back my phone. I shoved it into my pocket. "We can still have dinner. It's not like there is much we can do about the bounty right this moment."

Maciah glanced at the two covered trays, then back at me. "There's always something." His tone was solemn, and I regretted telling him about the reward before eating. It wasn't like he'd truly enjoy the food, but this would have been the first time we were together and didn't spend most of it arguing about all the crap going on around us.

I lifted the tray, trying to get him excited again. Underneath were steaks, fresh bread, and veggies. My face scrunched in confusion, then Maciah lifted the other lid.

"This one was a joke," he said, nodding toward the Hot Pockets.

I smiled. "It was funny. I laughed pretty hard."

He put the cover back down and grabbed my hand. "I know. I could hear from the hallway. I'm glad. You should do that more often."

"Laugh? Our lifestyle doesn't often give moments of laughter," I said.

"Then, we should do something about that."

I nodded. "But after we eat. Now that I can smell the steaks over the frozen crap, I'm starving."

Maciah released my hand and made us two plates. I was going to gain fifty pounds if I stayed in this mansion for long. Between Nikki's cooking over the last couple of days and this dinner, I'd eaten more lately than I normally did in an entire week.

We sat on the couch, and Maciah lifted the top of the coffee table up so that we could eat without bending over.

"Fancy," I said with a grin.

"It comes in handy when I can't leave my office," Maciah replied, cutting into his steak.

The inside of his was raw. Like all the way. Only the outside had been seared, and I tried not to be grossed out by it, considering I knew humans who ate their meat the same way.

Mine was a medium rare which was surprisingly how I preferred it. I had no idea how Maciah had managed to get dinner up here so quickly, but I didn't question things. He'd made the effort, and I wasn't going to try to ruin it again.

"Besides the courtyard, did you find enough to do around here to keep you busy the last couple of days?" Maciah asked. He was trying to make small talk. It was adorable.

"The gym is pretty awesome. Other than that, I spent most of my time outside or with Rachel and Nikki who warned me not to go to the cabin areas where you were."

He grimaced. "While I trust all of the vampires that live on this property to an extent, they were right to caution you. When we have a newborn, the others get a little jumpy. Add you to the mix and they're more on guard than normal. I'll take you out there whenever you'd like, though. There is nothing here that is off limits to you."

Well, that was nice of him.

We ate in silence for several minutes, and I took a drink of my water, noticing he didn't have any blood to drink. "You know it doesn't bother me if you eat from a glass, right?"

"I drank enough after my shower." He smiled, showing off a small dimple I hadn't noticed before.

We continued to chat idly about nothing and anything. It was odd, but welcoming.

I never imagined I'd befriend a vampire, let alone be attracted to one or have dinner with him.

Life had a way of stirring things up when I least expected it, and even though there was a reward for my capture and two old and powerful vampires were after me for various reasons, I was content for the first time in much too long.

21

TWO WEEKS HAD PASSED SINCE I'D MOVED INTO THE vampire nest. The first week was rough, but the second was a little easier. I began trusting the vampires around me a little more and doing my best to accept what my life had become.

Maciah and I continued to have our dinners. Sometimes alone, sometimes with Rachel, Nikki, and Zeke. I was getting antsy, though. I was used to hunting nearly every night. Sitting around, playing games, working out—none of it was curbing my appetite for justice.

I was in my room, organizing my stakes and daggers that really didn't need to be organized when a knock sounded.

Rachel's head poked in as I turned around. "Hey, are you busy?"

I laughed. "I haven't been busy since I moved into this place."

She grinned widely. "Well, hopefully that's about to change. Come on. Zeke said he has some news."

"What news?" I asked.

"I don't know. That's why we need to hurry," she said, grabbing on to my hand as I dropped a couple stakes back into the drawer where I kept them.

We rushed down the hallway. I'd been working on my running, trying to draw on whatever skills I was supposed to be acquiring even as a mortal. My speed had increased, but not as much as I'd hoped.

Nikki was already in the office when we arrived, along with Zeke and Maciah. Nobody seemed upset, so I took that as a good thing.

I chose to stand while Rachel sat next to Nikki. Maciah nodded at me, his eyes darkening as he appraised me. He did so openly and often in front of all of his vampires. I wasn't sure how I would feel about that at first, but the more he made me feel for him, the less I cared what others might think.

I smiled in return when Maciah didn't seem to be able to look away from me. Finally, Zeke spoke up, breaking whatever awkwardness Maciah and I were creating for everyone else.

"Amersyn, I know you've been feeling trapped here. We all appreciate how accepting you've been of the changes thrown at you. So, as a thank you for your cooperation, I've been working on something. I didn't want to say anything in case I came up empty-handed, but I have news." The vampire's smile stood out brightly against his dark skin, and he was practically bouncing in his seat.

"Is Silas or Viktor dead? Even better, both of them?" I asked.

"No, but this might be just as good for you," he responded.

I narrowed my eyes at him. "Spit it out already, dude." I wasn't the most patient person in the world.

"I found out where Rigo is going to be tomorrow. Somewhere I think we can get close to him," Zeke said.

My heart raced as the news sank in. A giddiness came over me, and I nearly squealed with joy. "Seriously? Like you know exactly where he'll be and what time and everything?"

He nodded, still grinning. "Seriously. It's his two-hundredth birthday, and he wanted to celebrate big in Vegas. Apparently, that got shut down by another big nest there and his party has been moved to Los Angeles. With the time we have to prepare, I think we can put together a plan solid enough that the risk will be minimal."

Maciah still hadn't spoken or moved from his spot. He didn't seem nearly as thrilled about this news as I was, and I wasn't sure why.

I glanced at him, and he was staring down at his desk. "What do you think?" I asked him.

"I think that this is something you've been wanting, and we should do it if that's what you still want," Maciah replied, his words sounding almost rehearsed.

"Of course, it's what I want. This bastard played a

role in killing my family. He needs to die," I said defensively.

"I agree," Maciah replied.

"But?" I pressed. I didn't want to fight with Maciah. We'd been getting along so well. Except I could tell he wasn't happy with something.

"The protector in me wants to keep you here forever, but I know I can't do that. I'm going to support whatever choice you make."

"Choice? Like I have options here? He has to die, Maciah," I said, hating that I was beginning to second-guess myself. Was I being selfish for wanting to go after another vampire when we already had two that wanted me dead?

No, I needed this. There was no reason to waver on this decision. Zeke had put forth the effort, and we were going to kill Rigo. Tomorrow.

Holy shit. I was going to kill another of the five tomorrow. I wasn't sure how I was going to contain my excitement, and Maciah's hesitancy wasn't going to ruin this for me. He might not like the thought of leaving his mansion, but as he'd said, it was just the protector in him.

Finding Rigo was exactly what I needed to feel better about everything that had been happening. We hadn't received word about Silas in days, and Viktor or his crew hadn't been sighted since that initial visit to the bar that Dave had told me about.

My bartender had been checking in with me, but things had remained unusually quiet. I knew that couldn't be good, but there was nothing I could do about it given my current situation.

Rigo, though? He was something I couldn't ignore. Plus, it was all the way in LA. By the time word got out that we'd been in town, it would be too late for anyone to do anything. We'd show up at the party, I'd kill the vampire, and then we'd come home.

Home. Huh. I hadn't realized I was beginning to consider the nest home. I wasn't sure how I felt about that, but analyzing that could wait.

"So, where is this party at?" I asked, needing more details so I could begin formulating my plan.

"It's at a supernatural club called Warlock. Normally, it's for humans and supernaturals, but it will only be open to invited guests tomorrow. There's a bouncer there named Gregory who we can trust. He'll get us in, no problem, as long as Rigo doesn't replace the staff for the night," Zeke answered.

"And what is the plan if the staff is replaced?" Maciah asked, taking a seat at his desk.

"Then, I get us in," I said. I already knew how this would work. I always had back-up plans.

Maciah raised a brow at me. "How so?"

"I'm still human. You might sense the vampire in me, but that's because we're linked. Nobody else knew before you said anything, right?" I asked.

Maciah grimaced. He was a smart man. He knew where I was going. "No, they didn't, but that doesn't mean older, more powerful vampires won't realize what you're up to or, even worse, recognize you. There is a bounty out on you, Amersyn. We don't know how far word has spread about that."

"I can wear a wig and pile on the makeup. It's amazing what some contouring can do to a girl," I said with a smile.

Maciah wasn't going to win this. He had to support me. We'd made a deal. Sure, that was before I accepted my heritage and before we knew about Viktor, but I couldn't let this opportunity pass by. It would shatter me.

"Okay," Maciah said.

"Okay? Just okay? No other counter arguments?" I asked.

"Nope."

I glanced at the others, wondering what they were thinking. Nikki just shrugged, and Rachel was avoiding my stare. Zeke seemed to be the most supportive, and I wasn't sure why. I was grateful but curious at the same time.

"Fine. When do we leave?" I asked.

"Tomorrow morning. I'll have a plane ready. We will drive in one car with all of us sitting in the back behind tinted windows and another vampire driving. The plane will take us to a private airstrip outside of LA, and then we'll head to my house there and regroup, depending on how things go up until that point," Maciah answered.

For someone who didn't seem to be fond of the idea of leaving, he sure seemed to have a solid itinerary laid out already.

"Thank you, Maciah," I said sincerely. He wasn't holding me back from my purpose, even though things were uncertain around us. That made my attraction to him go up a few levels. A man that could stand beside his woman instead of in front of or behind her was a man worthy of her heart.

"I'm going to go check on a few other pieces of information and make sure nothing has changed," Zeke said.

I reached for him as he passed me. "Thank you as well. I didn't expect to get this opportunity until the other things were dealt with. It means more to me than I can express."

"Honestly, I expected you to kill us all. The fact that you didn't and have embraced everything around you deserves something in return," he said.

I laughed. "I'm not sure how I should take that."

Zeke grinned. "Good. I like to keep people on their toes. Makes life interesting."

The vampire left. Nikki got up next with Rachel right behind her. "If we're going to a club, I need to pick out some outfits. Don't worry, I'll get you something to wear, too," Nikki said to me.

"I think that worries me more," I replied with a wink.

Rachel gave me a hug. "This is good news. Just remember that."

They left the office, and Rachel's ominous words didn't have me feeling much better. I wasn't sure what to do next.

When I'd entered the room, the attraction between Maciah and I was tangible, but now...I didn't know how okay Maciah really was with the plan. Given that I wasn't one to ignore problems, I turned toward Maciah after closing his door.

"Tell me how you really feel about this little side mission," I said as I walked toward his desk and rested against it while facing him.

He pushed his chair back so he could look up at me better. "This is what you've been wanting. I don't see how you'll get another opportunity like this."

"Those are facts. Not how you feel. Don't get me wrong, I can't ignore this, but I'd like to know your concerns before we go. If there are certain things that we can avoid doing to lessen the risks, we will, but if you don't tell me what you believe those are, then I won't know."

Maciah tugged me onto his lap, and I didn't fight him. I sat across him with my legs over the arm of the chair. His palm covered my leg as his thumb rubbed small circles on my inner thigh.

"When I first realized you existed and what was happening, I found every bit of information I could on what it meant to be a protector. I researched who you could be and whose child you might have been. I had very little information to go off since it was only your blood I scented, but the moment I saw you in that alley, I knew who you were."

"How?" I asked when he paused.

"Your eyes. You might think you had your

stepfather's eyes, but I believe your mother purposely searched for someone who resembled Darius. A task that had to break her heart but was necessary to keep you safe. You look just like the original vampire."

"Do you have a picture of him?" I hadn't asked before, because I hadn't been ready. I wished more than anything I could ask my mother these questions, but Maciah was going to be the closest I came to getting answers.

"I have a portrait from an old book. I'll grab it," he said, moving to lift me up.

I shook my head. "Later. I believe you, and I would rather continue the conversation about how you feel concerning this trip."

He settled back into his chair and wrapped his other arm around my back. "As your protector, it's my job to keep you away from danger. As someone who cares about you, it's also my job to make sure you're happy. I know as the days pass and you stay locked up here, that happiness is harder to grasp. I can't properly explain how I feel about this trip, because there are two halves of me at war right now."

I reached up, grabbing his neck. "You have no idea how much I appreciate that you're not letting the protector in you stop me from doing what I need. What can I do to make this easier on you?"

I might have only known Maciah less than a few weeks, and I might not have been a willing participant in everything to begin with, but the more I got to know him, the more I respected what he stood for and what he was trying to do.

"We need to know exactly what we're going to do and what we'll do when something doesn't go as planned. When we have that sorted out, then I can stop being as stressed," he replied.

"Understandable. How about we start plotting now?" I suggested.

He closed the small space between us and pressed his lips to mine. "I have several things we can plot."

His voice was playful, and I was glad I'd chosen to face him head-on instead of ignoring how he felt. We were adults, and with trust shared between us, we could finally act like it.

"Let's see how quickly we can sort out this Rigo adventure, and then I'm happy to hear your other ideas," I said before kissing him back.

His hands tightened around me. "We better hurry then."

22

MACIAH AND I LET OURSELVES GET DISTRACTED, BUT NOT for long. We invited the others back into the office and ordered food to be delivered. Pepperoni pizza with jalapenos, a favorite of mine and something Nikki also enjoyed, but the others all passed on the spicy toppings. I didn't mind, because when it came to pizza, my stomach had no limits.

"Damn, that was good," I groaned after my sixth slice.

Zeke frowned at me. "I miss enjoying food that much."

His words gave me pause. I didn't want to think about how my life would one day change. The more I got to know the vampires, the more unsure I was about what I planned to do after I died. My mind still agreed I needed to end my vampire existence after turning as quickly as possible, but my heart was growing fonder of Maciah and wanting more time with him. Only the future would tell what I would do.

"Doesn't blood give you a boost?" I finally asked.

Zeke was mid-sip—they'd gotten better about drinking around me, and I'd stopped being as grossed out—so Nikki answered instead. "It does, but not like drinking from a human. Don't get me wrong, I'm glad I don't do that. There were too many times that I lost control of myself due to the euphoria that races through us when we sink our fangs into flesh. I don't want to be a murderer. Though, there is nothing that can replicate the feeling."

Nikki's honesty took me a bit by surprise. The fact that they could control their thirst and ignore the desires they clearly got from drinking out of the proverbial tap was another reason I trusted them. Any vampire that had that much strength couldn't be all that bad.

"Maybe we can find you a life-like dummy and pump some blood through it," I joked, reaching for another slice of pizza, because why not.

She laughed. "I'm not sure it works that way, but good thought."

"Does everything feel good about our plans?" Rachel asked, giving me a pointed stare before taking the pizza box away.

I wanted to be mad, but she'd made the right move. I was going to be sick if I continued eating. It was just so damn good.

"Fang yes, we do," Zeke said, causing everyone else to laugh and me to groan.

"You guys have to let that go," I begged.

Rachel reached for me, grabbing my wrist. "Not a chance, Amersyn."

I turned away from her and found Maciah staring at me. His eyes were brown with only light touches of red, a color I noticed they took on when he was happy. Not aroused, but just enjoying life in the moment. It was a color I liked. A lot.

"Fine. Have your fun. At my expense. I'll try not to make your deaths slow when I lose my shit," I replied with a smile.

None of them seemed at all afraid of my loosely given threat. We'd moved beyond that, and they knew it.

"But yes, the plan is solid. Rigo will die tomorrow," Maciah said confidently.

We would fly out at five the next morning and arrive in LA just a couple hours later. Apparently, Maciah had houses all over the West Coast and a few scattered around other areas of the United States. Once we got to his house, we would check in with Gregory, the bouncer, to make sure everything was still good to go.

The next part I wasn't worried about, but Maciah was. It involved me spending the rest of the day being turned into a hooker. Okay, I probably wouldn't look like I was for sale, but I was going to be dressed up with full make-up, a wig, and an outfit that left little to the imagination with the hope that Rigo picked me out of the crowd to spend time with.

I'd have stakes hidden on me and, best-case scenario, get Rigo by himself and finish him off before doing our best to sneak away. The getaway part was the only piece of the plan that had too many variables. We'd have our exits planned out of the city, but we'd have to wing it from the club.

If Rigo didn't pick me out of the crowd, I'd shove myself at him, which would be more suspicious, but it was really the only other option.

If I couldn't get him alone, I'd have to publicly seduce him, which I wasn't fond of, and neither was Maciah. I was pretty sure he was trying to pretend I wasn't about to throw myself at another man, something he wouldn't be able to ignore if it was happening in front of him.

Lastly, if all those other things failed, we'd wait him out. The party had to end at some point. We'd get inside to see how many guards Rigo had with him and what kind of fight we'd be getting into. Either way, we weren't walking away without at least making an attempt to end Rigo.

For two-hundred years, he'd terrorized humans. I couldn't let that go on any longer. My family—and all the others he'd ruined before and after murdering mine—deserved that justice, even if they never knew it happened.

Nikki stood, breaking my thoughts away from the plan we'd been over several times throughout the night.

She groaned and stretched. "I'm going to go make sure all my stuff is accounted for. Morning is going to come soon."

"Don't remind me. I know we don't need sleep, but I do enjoy it still." Rachel stood to leave as well, and Zeke followed them out.

"We'll see you guys in the morning," he said.

"Goodnight," I replied, then turned to Maciah. "I should head to bed, too. I actually do need sleep to function tomorrow."

"Will you stay with me tonight?" he asked, voice soft, almost as if he was unsure of himself.

We'd spent many late nights staying up together, talking and kissing, but not much else. I wasn't in a hurry when it came to Maciah. The slow burn simmering between us felt perfect, but the thought of having him hold me all night... I couldn't think of any reason to turn that down.

"I would love to," I replied.

Maciah got up, taking calculated steps toward me. I had no idea what he was up to, but I wasn't going to complain. Especially not when his eyes darkened, and he stared at me as if nothing else in the world mattered.

He bent down and picked me up from where I'd been sitting in the chair. I dropped the slice of pizza I'd taken but not eaten onto the coffee table and gave Maciah my full attention as he cradled me in his arms.

I'd thought I would hate being carried, that it would seem as if the person doing so thought I was incapable in some way, but as Maciah's grip tightened on me, none of those thoughts entered my mind.

He might have been bound to protect me from the dangers that lurked in the shadows, but taking care of me like he had been had nothing to do with protection. That was about attraction and affection, two things I never would have assumed vampires were capable of, but Maciah and the others I'd gotten to know were proving me wrong about a lot of things on a daily basis.

For once, I had no problem being wrong.

Maciah carried me out of the office, then grinned down at me. "Hold on tight."

I was confused until the walls became a blur and my stomach nearly came up out of my throat. Before I knew it, he was opening his door and gently setting me down on his bed.

"Don't…ever…do that…again," I moaned.

"If you hadn't eaten so much, you wouldn't feel so sick," he teased.

He might have been right, but I hadn't known he was going to race across the house with me without much notice.

The room only spun for a moment before I was able to look up at him again without wanting to be sick.

When my eyes met his, they were scrunched. "I'm sorry. I didn't actually think it would affect you that badly."

"I'm fine." I waved him off and stood, then wobbled.

Maciah caught my arms, holding me close. "Do you want me to go get your pajamas?" he asked.

Well, how was I supposed to answer that question? The only time I'd slept in clothes at the mansion was when Rachel was watching over me. Even then it was the shirt I'd worn that day and my underwear. I didn't actually own any pajamas. Something I hadn't really thought about when I agreed to stay in his room for the night.

"Um, no. I'm good. I'll sleep in what I have," I said, avoiding his gaze.

He held me tighter. "You know I remember everything about the night I broke into your house. Not a detail has escaped me."

I tried not to laugh as I remembered getting out of my bed naked without a care in the world. Yeah, he'd gotten an eyeful.

"Is that so?" I hoped he didn't think I was getting naked now. I wasn't diving into the deep end that fast.

His hands traveled down my arms, then up my waist until he held my face. "Every curve and mark on your body, Amersyn."

Damn, that was hot.

My fingers gripped his shirt tighter as I pressed myself closer to him. I needed to be patient. I was not sleeping with him after only knowing him a few weeks. I had to keep my resolve.

Yes, I was also aware I was an idiot.

This man was sexy, caring, and wanted me. Still, something held me back. I didn't know what it was, but it wasn't often that I ignored my instincts. They rarely led me wrong.

"How about I settle for one of your shirts as pajamas?" I suggested, then added, "That is, if you own t-shirts."

Maciah smirked at me. "I have everything you will ever need."

I didn't miss the underlying promise in his words as I followed him to his walk-in closet. He opened the door, and it was exactly as I expected. Rows of black to grey suits, crisp white dress shirts, a handful of sweaters and khaki-type pants, along with one section of military-style clothing like I'd seen him wearing the first night in the alley.

In one of the drawers beneath the racks, he pulled out a plain white tee. It was going to fall to my knees, but that was probably for the best.

He handed me the shirt. "Bathroom is the next door over."

I nodded and took the clothing before heading directly for the bathroom. I'd never been ashamed of my body, but I knew if I got naked in front of Maciah, any thoughts of keeping things slow would go out the window.

As quickly as I could, I undressed until all that was left was my underwear, which thankfully covered most of my ass. I slipped the shirt over my head and groaned. My nipples were on full display through the thin material.

Of course, he only has white shirts, I thought.

I went to the sink and stole some of his toothpaste to put on my finger that would sub as my toothbrush. Not ideal, but it would be good enough until morning when I went back to my room to get ready.

After I "brushed" my teeth, I decided to wash my face. Then, I eyeballed the shower that had four shower heads and fluffy white towels folded on a shelf next to it.

I shook my head. I was stalling. I'd never done that before. We were only going to sleep. I didn't need to be so nervous.

I gathered my resolve and headed out of the bathroom. Maciah was already under his silk black sheets with the lights off except the lamp next to him.

Any nerves I'd had before were gone as his dark eyes met mine. He lifted the sheet, and I saw he wore loose sleep pants and nothing else.

My steps were slow as I appraised him. I'd yet to see him with his shirt off and that was probably a good thing. His chest was defined by lines that showcased his time in the gym. He had a solid six-pack—nothing over the top, but there was no denying his strength, even without the vampire benefits.

There was a tattoo above his heart. The very spot I'd wanted to stab when I first met him. As I crawled onto the bed, my fingers reached for the black ink. It reminded me of a Celtic knot at first, but on closer inspection, the lines also made me think of a man's chest with his arms crossed, holding two blades. Nothing distinctive, just the perfectly drawn lines making that the first thought that came to mind as I traced over the ink.

"What does it mean?" I asked, settling into bed next to Maciah and laying on my side so I could face him.

He lowered his head to the pillow, doing the same as me. "Nothing official, but for me, it reminds me of the strength I need to keep moving forward. No matter how impossible it seems to find a way back to the old ways of our kind, I can't stop fighting for that."

My hand cupped his cheek, and he brought his face closer to mine. "Then, it's the perfect tattoo for you," I said.

"What about yours?" he asked, lifting the sleeve to show my tribal marks.

"I don't know. I'd asked the artist to draw me something that would remind me of vengeance. When he showed me the art, I just knew it was right."

"You have good instincts." He kissed me, and I tried to tug him closer, but he pulled back. "You need rest for tomorrow," he reminded me.

Taking things slow had never seemed more idiotic, but as I agreed and rolled over, I was more content than ever before. Maciah wrapped his arms around me, making me feel safe and cared for.

23

EARLY MORNING CAME QUICKLY, BUT I WASN'T complaining. As I headed back to my room, all I could think about was the fact that I was going to bring another murderer to justice by the day's end.

As I closed the door behind me, I took a deep breath and pictured my family. I hoped they'd be proud of what I'd become, of what I was fighting for and doing.

Maciah had been right when I'd first met him. I was searching for vengeance. But, I had no plans to get off this path once the vampires I searched for were dead. Other families deserved someone to fight for them as well.

I walked to my closet with my mother, father, and brother still heavy on my mind, as I knew they would be all day, but thoughts of my night with Maciah weren't far behind them.

He'd remained the perfect gentleman as we lay in bed together all night. His arms never left me, and when I thought I would get tired of the constant touch, I only wanted more from him.

I got dressed, amazed at how much life had changed in the last few weeks. I'd been so afraid that by accepting these vampires and accepting that I would one day become one of them that it would change who I was at my core, but none of that had happened.

Even though not much time had passed, I already knew that Maciah, Rachel, Nikki, and Zeke would never expect me to be someone I wasn't. They would support my decisions and desires. That fact had been proven when Zeke took it upon himself to search for the vampires that I still wanted dead.

I'd never asked him to do that, especially not when we had other threats to worry about. Still, they'd kept my wants at the forefront of their thoughts and were following through, even when it wasn't exactly safe to do so.

We had plenty to worry about. Just because I was going to be wearing a disguise, didn't mean that nobody would realize who I was, but that was a risk we were all willing to take.

I grabbed my stuff and headed back toward my door. As I grasped the handle, it was already turning. I stepped back to find Rachel getting ready to walk in.

"I was just coming to see if you needed help, but I see you're all set," she said with a smile.

"That I am. Is everyone else ready?" I asked, meeting her in the hallway before closing my door.

She nodded. "Zeke is warming up the SUV. Eddie is

going to be driving us. Maciah and Nikki should be out any minute."

A shift in the air had me turning around to find Maciah right behind her. "Good morning," he said casually.

"It is a good morning, isn't it?" Rachel added. She was almost as excited about hunting down Rigo as I was.

Maciah winked at me. "Yes, it is. Where's Nikki?"

"Down here." She was waiting at the bottom of the stairs wearing sweatpants, slippers, and a sweatshirt. I should have copied her.

We got to the first floor and headed toward the garage. The door was open, and an icy blast cut right through me. "Mother effer, it's freezing out here."

"Yeah, it's beginning to snow. We need to hurry to the airstrip before it's too icy to take off. They don't have the same resources there as they do at the main terminals," Maciah said.

My steps quickened, and I threw my bag into the waiting SUV before climbing into the back seat. Rachel and Nikki joined me while Maciah and Zeke took the middle. Eddie was already in the driver's seat and turned around to face us.

"Morning, everyone," he said before putting the vehicle in reverse. Eddie's auburn hair was combed and still wet from a recent shower. He wore a forest-green jacket and dark-wash jeans, looking more put together than when I normally saw him either coming in from dealing with newborns or in the gym.

Everyone was tense on the way to the airstrip. We watched as the snow continued to fall and began sticking to the ground. Every minute that passed had me more worried we weren't going to get to LA when we needed to. This was the opportunity we needed to get one of the elusive Russian vampires. I couldn't fathom having all of our plans ruined by the damn weather.

Thirty long minutes later, Eddie pulled into the parking lot, as close to the gate as he could get us. We raced out of the SUV and grabbed our things.

Zeke took my bag and Rachel took Maciah's. "We're going to need to run," Zeke said.

Before I could respond, Maciah picked me up and the world around us became a blur. I hadn't eaten breakfast, so the uneasiness I'd felt last time didn't come, but with the chill, I still found it hard to breathe when he sat me down at the base of the plane stairs.

A pilot dressed in a blue uniform was waiting for us. "We have maybe a minute to start taxiing before we get shut down."

Nobody questioned him. We rushed the rest of the way onto the aircraft and got seated in the ten-passenger plane. There was nothing overly fancy inside: just a few rows of seats, the cockpit, a bathroom, and a small storage area where our bags had been tossed.

"We made it," Nikki said as we all buckled up.

"You're going to jinx us," Zeke replied as the plane started to move.

I didn't say a word and hardly took a breath until

we started to pick up speed. Even then, I was tense. We were flying through a snowstorm. I was the only human on the plane. Sure, I'd turn into a vampire if I died, but I definitely wasn't ready for that.

"Don't worry. If the plane goes down, I'll get to the ground first and catch you," Maciah whispered in my ear.

"Not helping," I replied through clenched teeth as turbulence was already rocking the plane.

He took my hand and rubbed his thumb over my palm. I closed my eyes and did my best to only focus on his touch, even as my seat shook so hard my bones felt like they'd been rattled.

WHEN WE ARRIVED IN LA, THE SUN WAS OUT, AND THE temperature was in the sixties. Freaking lucky Californians.

The drive to Maciah's house wasn't too bad, even with morning traffic. As we pulled up, I wasn't surprised to find a mini version of his home back in Portland.

There was an iron fence covered in ivy around the property and a hand imprint was needed to get in. The gates opened, and the driveway led us to a white home about a third of the size as the mansion, but still beautiful.

There were two columns holding up the front porch. It had a red front door and flowers planted around the house. They were peonies in varying shades of red, pink, orange, and white. A better choice than the roses, in my opinion.

"I haven't been here in so long," Rachel said as she got to the door first.

"I checked on everything when I was visiting my sister. It's still in good shape. The rental company has been keeping it stocked with food, too," Nikki said.

As we walked in, I asked, "Is the person you call your sister actually your sister?"

Nikki shook her head. "We were both turned around the same time. She escaped before me but had tried to get me out as well. She leads a different life than we do at Maciah's, but she doesn't kill humans."

Hmm, as far as Nikki knew, she didn't, but I didn't say my thoughts out loud. We had bigger problems to worry about.

"Grab whatever rooms you want to get ready in. Amersyn and I will take my normal room. The vampires driving down to join us won't be sleeping or needing to get ready, so don't worry about them," Maciah said, and I turned toward him.

I grabbed his hand as the others moved on. "Umm, what vampires driving down?"

"I have twenty of our regulars driving down from Portland. They left late last night and will be here this afternoon," he replied as if it wasn't a big deal.

"Why didn't I know we had extra people coming?" I asked, feeling like this was indeed a big deal and something that should have been talked about the couple of times we solidified our plans.

"Zeke thought of it yesterday. I let him take care of things and forgot about it. In case things go wrong at the club, we'll have people we can trust nearby to help us. What's wrong with that?" he asked.

I wasn't sure. There was no reason for me to be making a big deal out of not knowing, but something about having so many of the nest with us didn't sit right with me. Maybe I was worried we'd draw too much attention or something. I didn't know.

"I guess nothing. I was just surprised to hear you say that," I said, then remembered the other thing. "Also, as much as I enjoyed last night, I'd still like to have my own room if we're staying the night."

Maciah smiled and reached for my hand. "At the nest, you can, but while we're here, I'd feel better having you close. The others understand that as well. I can sleep in the chair if that would make you feel better, but I doubt we'll even be here long enough to worry about that. The only reason we'd have to stay is if we can't land in Portland."

"You definitely won't be sleeping in a chair," I said, glad he understood and didn't seem to take offense to my objection.

He led us toward a downstairs master suite. There was nothing fancy or remarkable about the room. That seemed to be the theme of the whole house. While the property was in pristine condition on the outside, there was nothing that had stood out to me when we walked inside.

Maciah had my bag and set it down. "If you want to get any more sleep, you can do so now. We won't be leaving here until late tonight."

"I'm good." My phone buzzed, distracting me.

Pete: I don't know how, but I received keys and the deed to a new gym in South Portland. If you need somewhere to stay still, there's a place for you here.

A map link followed with the address, and I stared up at Maciah. "Did you buy Pete a new gym?"

He shrugged, not answering me with words.

I reached for him. "Why?"

"Because the thought of him being hurt upset you. I didn't want you to feel guilty."

Words were lost on me. I didn't know what to say. The gesture was huge and showed me another layer of Maciah that had my heart opening to him.

I tightened my hold on him. "Thank you."

"You're welcome." He looked around, seeming very uncomfortable talking about his good deed. "Do you need anything?"

"Do you have coffee in this place?" I asked, still amazed by his kindness.

"We do. I pay a property management company to come in and clean this place once a month and bring in fresh food for times we need to stay here without much notice," he answered.

"Practical vampire," I teased.

He grabbed my hips, pulling me toward him. "Is 'prick' officially out of my title now?"

I chuckled. "Not permanently, but I'll keep that name reserved for special occasions, so you know just how mad I am when I use it."

Maciah's lips pressed to mine as he smiled. "Good to know. Now, let's go get you some caffeine."

Following him out of the room, I pushed away any earlier worries about arriving vampires and the impending death of Rigo.

For the moment, everything was fine, and I wanted to revel in that.

Night had fallen, and I'd been transformed into a new identity. Hours had been spent on my make-up and finding the perfect outfit to go with the short auburn wig Nikki had brought for me to wear.

When I'd looked at myself in the mirror, I didn't recognize the face in the reflection. My normally fair skin had more color to it from foundation and a spray-on tan. My cheekbones were highlighted with blush, and my eyes were covered in blue contacts with shimmering eyeshadow on my lids.

The dress I'd squeezed into was a black number covered in lace. It was tight, but long enough that I could keep some shorter modified stakes strapped to each of my thighs, as well as a few more in my knee-high boots.

I'd yet to see Maciah since Rachel and Nikki finished working on me. There was a knock at Rachel's bedroom door, and I tensed, wondering if it was him.

Instead, Zeke walked in with a hand over his eyes. "Is everyone decent?"

Rachel giggled and Nikki threw a pillow at him. "Yes, weirdo."

When his hand came down, he let out a whistle as he appraised the three of us. "You ladies are... I'm not even sure if I can say the words I'm thinking. Just know you're looking good, but damn, Amersyn. Maciah isn't going to let you into that club."

Yeah, I was a little worried that maybe we'd done too good of a job on my makeover.

Rachel shushed him. "He will if he knows what is good for him."

"I was just coming to let you ladies know that the other vampires are in place and we're ready to go when you are," Zeke said.

"Where is Maciah?" I asked.

"He was speaking with the few assigned group leaders we have. Don't worry. He's been missing you all day, Hunter," Zeke replied.

I felt a little uncomfortable. Sure, the three of them knew there was something going on between Maciah and me, but it hadn't really been talked about openly. I wasn't much of a sharer, and Rachel and Nikki thankfully hadn't pried after the first time.

When the room became awkward from my lack of response, Zeke backed toward the door. "I guess we'll see you downstairs, then."

I sighed. I was not good at this relationship thing.

Nikki patted my arm. "Don't worry. Maciah won't

stop the plan, and you don't need to talk about anything that you don't want to."

"But we're here if you do want to, because we're good listeners and would never share anything you tell us in private," Rachel added quickly.

I smiled at them both. "Thank you. Seriously, I didn't know what to expect coming into this situation. I thought I would be miserable, but you ladies have made sure that wasn't the case."

"We've been at this womance thing for a while. We know how to read people, and we'll never push you for more than you're ready for," Nikki replied.

"Womance? Is that the female equivalent to bromance?" I joked.

"Damn right, it is," Rachel said proudly.

I grinned widely. "I'm honored to be part of your womance, then."

We gathered into a group hug, standing together for only a few seconds, but they were impactful ones. It wasn't just Rachel's and Nikki's words that made me trust them, but their actions. I had always been a singular-focus person. Having people around me who understood that and didn't expect more out of me than what I was capable of was exactly what I needed.

"It's nearly ten. We should get going," Nikki said.

Tension tightened in my shoulders as I nodded. Going on hunts was something that had become the norm for me over the years. I'd done the disguise thing before—though, not as elaborate as I was done up now—and I'd ended at least two of my family's murderers, but something about this made me feel different.

Maybe it was that I was different. I knew that while I still believed and wanted the same things that nothing was the same, either. I wanted to end the vampires I hunted, but I also was aware that not all of them were killers like I'd previously thought.

Rachel and Nikki waited for me at the doorway. I took a deep breath and joined them, feeling better with them at my side.

We headed into the living room. Maciah's back was to us, and Rachel cleared her throat. His phone slid into his pocket as he turned around and took all three of us in.

My eyes locked with Maciah's, sending heat straight to my core. He stalked toward me with lowered eyes. Rachel and Nikki left me standing there alone like traitors. So much for our womance.

Maciah's hand raised, brushing lightly over my left cheek, then down my arm. He grabbed my hand, bringing it to his lips. "Stunning," he murmured, then, leaning in closer, "but I prefer the you I woke up next to this morning."

Mother eff. I didn't actually believe swooning was a real thing, but Maciah's words—along with his closeness, and the heat in his dark, appraising eyes— sucked the air right from my lungs.

"Thankfully, all this comes off. Well, hopefully," I finally said, hoping to diffuse the sexual tension growing around us, given we had an audience in the room.

"I'm happy to help with the task," he said with a grin.

My cheeks warmed as images of Maciah undressing me ran through my mind. Yeah, that was something to look forward to—a celebration after Rigo was turned to ash.

"The car is out front. Let's get out of here," Zeke said from the open door.

I straightened my shoulders and pushed naked thoughts out of my head as Maciah took my hand. Rachel and Nikki were grinning like fools until I glared at them, then they began laughing their asses off. Maybe that was why I never really had friends before meeting them.

In all fairness, if it was one of them in my position, I'd have been acting the same, so I couldn't really be mad at them.

There was a blacked-out Tesla crossover sitting in the driveway with the doors open and waiting. The car looked like a bird with its back doors up in the air, but I knew it would fit in with the area, so I kept my opinions to myself.

Maciah helped me into the back before sliding into the driver's seat. Part of the plan was for him to play driver/security guard to the three of us. Zeke was also security. Both of them grabbed hats from the dashboard they must have tossed up there earlier and pulled them low over their eyes, getting into character before we arrived.

They wore matching grey slacks and black dress shirts, something that could pass for a uniform of sorts if questioned about why they were there. I was the human plaything to Rachel and Nikki that was hoping to offer herself up to the guest of honor.

They wore silver dresses that swooped almost to their asses in the back and remained tight around the front. They were both stunning, but that was no surprise to me.

Maciah drove away from the house, and I watched as the city lights came into view. I hadn't been to Los Angeles before. I'd always wanted to go as a kid and visit Disneyland, but that never happened.

My eyes were glued to the passing of buildings and dirty streets. The further we drove in, the less I understood why people wanted to live in this craphole.

"The beach cities are much better than this. I'll take you to my favorites one day," Nikki said, and I nodded. I could go for a vacation as soon as there weren't vampires trying to kill me.

We pulled up to a brick building with a red carpet out front, ropes forming lines along the side, and one bouncer in the front.

A small valet stand was to the left of the door, and two younger men were working there. One of them approached the door, and it was time for our show.

Maciah and Zeke opened their doors at the same

time and pressed a button up front that lifted our doors as well.

The valet held his hand out to me. "Welcome to Warlock, miss."

I smiled at him and accepted the gesture, pretending to act amazed by the grandeur around me. "Thank you so much."

Nikki slid out behind me, and Rachel exited on the other side. I stayed between them as we walked the red carpet with Maciah and Zeke at our backs.

The bouncer made eye contact with Zeke and nodded, making me assume he was Gregory. "Are you here for the private event tonight?"

"We are," Nikki said.

"Names?" he asked after picking up a clipboard from behind him.

Rachel pointed at herself, then me and Nikki. "Sara, Brea, and Trixie."

Nikki's grip tightened around my elbow as Rachel said Trixie for her, and it took everything in me not to laugh.

Gregory scrolled his list, scratching out a few names, then writing a note. "Have fun, ladies." He lifted the red velvet rope, and we entered the club.

I kept a smile plastered to my face as my eyes roamed the room. The lights were dim, but the place wasn't overly crowded, so it was easy to see to the other side where I found a door swinging open that appeared to lead outside with two tall and glowering vampires guarding it.

"We need to get back there," I said.

"We will. Eventually," Nikki said.

I knew we couldn't seem too eager, but knowing I was in the same place as someone I'd wanted to kill for seven years? That had me on edge.

Maciah and Zeke stayed at the back wall, near others who appeared to be filling the same role of guard to others present.

I locked eyes with Maciah. His jaw was tight, and I knew it was hard for him to leave me alone in a room of supernaturals, but the fact that he was willing to do so... I wasn't going to forget that. Between his trust in me and the kind gestures he'd done since we'd met, I knew there was no going back.

If Maciah wanted me, then he could have me.

Rachel pulled me along when she noticed I'd stopped. "There are high-ranking vampires from all over. Even some shifters and witches are here, but not many. Rigo isn't well-liked by other races. Let's grab drinks first and scope out the bartender situation. Sometimes they're useful in parties like this."

A drink was exactly what I needed to calm my twitchy fingers.

We strolled up to the bar, giggling and falling over each other. The barkeep approached us with a grin on his face. "What can I get you ladies?"

Everything about the attractive man was dark except his light-green eyes. If I didn't have a sexy vampire waiting for me across the room, I might have hit on him. Instead, I let Nikki have her fun.

"Well, we just got here, and we need drinks. Real good ones, if you know what I mean. We're also hoping you can tell us where we can sign our friend up for donations," she said with a nod toward me.

He leaned against the bar top. "Well, it's a good thing you came to me. I can help you with both things. If you're here, then you know it's a special night for our guest of honor. He's the only one feeding, and you'll want to stand in that line over there to be picked out." He pointed toward a small section where there was already a massive line formed of waiting women.

There was something seriously wrong with every single one of them. Worse, it would take hours to *maybe* be seen. We were going to have to improvise, and we'd only just gotten here.

The bartender turned around to make us drinks, and Nikki nudged me. "Why don't you go get in line, *Brea*? We'll bring your drink over."

I was surprised she suggested I head off alone, but it wasn't like they'd be far away. I turned to head in that direction, but an old woman with silver hair and bright green eyes stepped into my path, looking past me at Rachel. "What are you doing here?" she demanded, magic pulsing off her.

"Something you don't need to worry about," Rachel said.

"I better not." The witch turned back to me, placing her hand over mine. A shock rolled through me. "How do you know Junie?" she asked.

I glanced back at Rachel and Nikki, wondering who the hell this lady was.

"Beatrix, she's human. Be easy on her," Rachel said.

The witch laughed. "Right. She carries magic from one of my witches who died during the last battle. I think that allows me a few questions."

Junie. She had to have been the witch I hoped to find that messed with my abilities.

"I didn't know her name was Junie. She went by J when I met her. I had actually wanted to see her again and ask her some questions. I'm sorry to hear she died," I answered sincerely.

The old woman appraised me again. "Interesting." She pulled a card from her loose cotton pants. "Come see me when you're done doing things I don't need to worry about and have time to visit."

I took the card and gladly slid it into the top of my dress. Beatrix was walking away before I could say anything else. "Do we need to be worried about her?" I asked.

Nikki shook her head. "She's just old and a little wacky. Go on ahead."

I didn't need to be told twice. I turned back toward the area the bartender had pointed at. The line was even longer as more people arrived. Damn. How many humans were invited to this thing? I probably didn't want to know.

Deciding I needed to make them see me a different way, I stole a drink from an empty table I passed and started to walk a little sideways as I approached the beginning of the line. My free hand moved over the wig, making sure it was still pinned on tight, then I bumped into the first human waiting.

She was a leggy blonde wearing a leather mini skirt and red corset top. Her blue eyes glared at me. "Watch where you're going, bitch."

I hiccupped dramatically, allowing my stolen drink to spill onto her skirt. "Oops. Let me get you a napkin." I giggled, moving out of her reach.

"I'm going to kill you," she screeched.

One of the bouncers made his way over to us. "I'm going to have to ask you both to leave."

My lower lip jutted out. "I'm so sorry. I didn't mean to cause any trouble."

The blonde launched herself at me. "You ruined everything!"

The bouncer grabbed her around the waist and picked her up as she continued to scream obscenities. He covered her mouth and headed toward the exit. Yeah, I probably just saved her life, and she had no clue.

"What's going on out here?" a deep, Russian voice sounded.

I turned around slowly, dropping the drunk girl act. "Oh, I'm so sorry to bother you, Rigo." I purred his name while also wanting to vomit.

His crimson eyes landed on me, trailing over my exposed skin. He licked his lips and crooked his finger at me. "Come here."

Every step I took was calculated. My hips swayed,

but not overly so. I bit my lip and kept my eyes lowered and submissive.

Rigo lifted my chin. "How come you're not in that line, beautiful?"

"Well, I just got here. I was making my way there," I replied softly.

"Nonsense. A treasure such as yourself shouldn't wait in lines," he said before picking me up and lifting me over the rope that blocked off the private area.

My stomach rolled as he set me back on my feet and grabbed my ass. "Get in there," he demanded.

I glanced back at the women still waiting. They were all glaring daggers and probably picturing ways they could kill me. I didn't care.

Nikki and Rachel approached the rope. They nodded at me as I turned around to enter the outdoor area. I might not have gotten in the way we planned, but the hard part was done.

Now, it was time for the dangerous part.

25

RIGO WRAPPED HIS FINGERS AROUND MY WRIST AND PULLED me into the patio area. There were two other vampires and another human female who was nearly passed out. Based on the puncture marks on her neck, that was likely from blood loss.

"What is your name?" Rigo asked me as he took a seat. He was dressed in an all-black suit. His dark hair was slicked back, making his cheekbones more prominent. He might sound Russian, but with his tanned skin and dark features, he was likely born elsewhere or once had parents that were.

I pressed my knees together, playing coy. "Brea."

"Well, Brea. Do you know what today is?" he asked.

I giggled. "It's your birthday."

His eyes darkened, and his legs spread open as he leaned back on the outdoor couch. "That's right. Did you bring me a present?"

My hands rubbed over my sides as I eyed the other men staring at me. "Maybe."

Rigo grabbed my hips and had me in his lap before I could try to do anything about being so close to him. "Show me."

"I've never done this before," I whispered.

Rigo raised his perfectly manicured hand up, fingers gripping my neck. "You're a feeder virgin?"

There was an excitement in his voice that gave me hope things were going to go exactly how I planned.

I nodded, eyes darting to the others again as I did my best to ignore the growing arousal beneath my ass.

"Are you shy, Brea?" he asked, squeezing tighter around my neck.

If I wasn't so sure he wanted to drink me dry, I'd have thought he was trying to kill me with his hold.

"Terribly so, but my friend told me I should find an experienced vampire for my first time. I didn't actually think I'd get the chance to meet you." I grabbed the lapels of his suit, running my fingers over the fine fabric.

"Well, it must be both of our lucky days." Rigo's head moved in close, and I nearly blew everything when I thought he was going to bite me. Before I could drop an elbow onto the back of his head, his tongue was the only thing I felt along my collarbone.

He turned toward the men still staring. "I'd like privacy with this one."

"Are you sure, boss?" one of them asked, but I was too busy playing meek to look up and see.

Rigo's hold on me tightened. "Absolutely. I want to take my time with the virgin."

Mother effer. I was going to be sick.

I kept my legs pressed together so that he wouldn't find my stakes before we were alone and lay my head against his chest. His hands splayed over my exposed upper back as he watched his men leave us alone.

When the door thudded closed, he lifted my head up to meet his gaze. "Where are you from, Brea?"

"Lynwood." It had been the name of the suburb where Maciah's house was. Hopefully that wasn't the wrong answer to give. As long as everything went as planned, he wouldn't be repeating the information anyway.

He picked up my wrist, smelling my veins. "There's something different about you."

Shit, that wasn't good.

"I hope that's a good thing. I'd hate to disappoint you," I cooed.

Rigo held my wrist painfully as he searched my face. "Yes, you would."

"I'd like to show you one of the gifts I have for you now," I said, hoping to distract him with thoughts of sex and blood.

He released me. "Present yourself to me."

This man was even more vile than I'd thought, but it was to my advantage.

I shoved him back, changing tactics and getting rough. "I heard you like a strong woman who can hold up to your needs."

He grinned. "Then, you heard right." I moved to get up, and he stopped me. "Where do you think you're going?"

"Don't you want to see what I have hiding under this dress?" I asked.

He nodded. "I could just rip it off."

"Then, our fun would be over much too soon," I countered.

"Very well. Proceed."

I stood up, glancing at the door to make sure it was all the way closed. The two men who had left even took the girl with them. I'd hoped to get her out when I left, but that wasn't going to happen.

There would only be one shot at killing Rigo. I had to make sure every move I made was one that brought me another step closer to ending him.

The music from inside played low on a speaker outside. I swayed my hips and moved closer to him again. My hands moved into the air, and I tilted my head back.

He reached for my thigh, and I smacked his hand unexpectedly. The move had him in my face, snarling. "Are you denying me?"

I smirked. "Not at all. I'm giving you a show."

"I've decided I don't want one," he said.

Using my enhanced strength, I shoved him back onto the couch and quickly kneeled before him. "Then, let me give you a different gift."

He seemed ready to backhand me until I started to unbuckle his pants. As his zipper came down, Rigo finally settled.

Before I could see something that I had no desire to, I reached down and grabbed one of my stakes. This was it. My one chance.

My free hand trailed up his chest, keeping him pressed against the couch as I leaned my head down, taking a deep breath.

His hips came up. "Get going before I change my mind. I'm not known for my patience."

"Yes, sir," I purred.

I leaped into his lap, straddling him, the stake now behind his head.

"This isn't the present I thought I was getting, but I am hungry." Rigo eyed my pulsing throat.

"Unfortunately, your last meal isn't going to be me," I said before leaning back and bringing the stake down, right into his chest with every ounce of strength I had in me.

His crimson eyes widened. "You…"

As I'd seen dozens of times before, his skin began to dry out and body shriveled. I got up, never once taking my eyes off of him until he turned to ash.

Freaking, disgusting vampire. I hadn't been sure he'd let me seduce him. That was what he got for thinking he was more powerful than he really was.

The dangerous part wasn't over, though. I had to get out of this area and back to the others without anyone realizing what I'd done until we were long gone.

There had been four guards—the two outside with

Rigo and the two blocking the door—assuming the one was back from kicking out the blonde.

I still had five stakes. That was more than enough, as long as I didn't draw any other attention.

I tightened my hold on the stake in my hand before cracking open the steel door. "Rigo is asking for one of you."

"Which one?" he grunted.

I couldn't see the other one next to him, so I yanked on his shirt. "You'll do."

He stumbled into the patio area as I closed the door behind him. He spun in a circle, searching for his boss.

I didn't wait for him to figure things out. I openly attacked him with a stake in my hand. He blurred out of the way before I made contact, then he reached for the door.

Letting him leave wasn't an option I could allow. I slammed into him, likely making too much noise. Spinning him around, I shoved him against the brick wall next to us.

His fist slammed into my jaw. My vision faltered, but my motivation didn't. I was getting out of this club alive.

He grabbed on to my neck, lifting me up until my feet dangled above the ground. "Where is Rigo?"

I didn't bother to answer him. He'd be seeing his boss soon enough in Hell. Ignoring the raging burn in my neck from his grip, I swung my legs up and kicked him in his chest.

He released me and my ankle cracked on the

concrete ground. I pushed through the pain, taking the opening I'd created. Somewhere, I'd dropped the stake I'd had, so I reached for another one, but he was already on me, fangs out and aimed for my neck.

I rolled out from under his hold and swung my armed hand up and around as I kicked him onto his back. The stake hit its mark perfectly as the brute bucked on the ground.

I stood up and struck my pointed boot into his ribs as payback for the bruises I was going to have courtesy of him. Though, the marks were also what I hoped would get me out of the bar without causing too big of a scene.

Reaching for another stake, I eyed the sharp tip, then without thinking too much, stabbed myself in the neck. Twice.

Nothing too deep, but enough to make me bleed and look close enough to bite marks. The wounds burned. Probably because of the silver. Having a reaction to silver was something I hadn't really wanted to accept before.

I unzipped one of my boots, taking it off and tossing it in the corner before rubbing dirt onto my clothes. I was officially a hot mess.

I forced tears to well in my eyes and let them fall down my bruised cheeks as I hobbled to the door. I opened it enough to slip through, sniffling as I shut it behind me.

Two of the three remaining guards were still there.

One of them smirked down at me with red eyes. "Have fun?"

I cowered beneath his stare and walked toward the rope.

One of the women waiting sneered at me. "That's what you get for cutting ahead of the rest of us."

Wow. Our world was turning to shit if that was truly what they thought when they saw another beaten woman. Seeing me should have made them run for the hills. Instead, they were glad I'd gotten what they thought I deserved.

Rachel and Nikki's faces came to view next. They wrapped an arm around me as I heard the patio door open. "Run," I said.

Nikki picked me up as we blurred through the club, pausing only long enough to make sure Maciah and Zeke were following us.

Shouts sounded behind us, and I was suddenly in Maciah's arms. "See you back at the house," he said to the others as we split up.

I hadn't liked this part of the plan, but I understood why it was necessary. My eyes closed as Maciah ran with me in his arms. His grip was tight, but not painfully so. I drew on his strength as the realization that I'd killed Rigo—and that we were getting away —hit me.

Images of my family were held firmly in my thoughts. I was another step closer to avenging them. Another murdering vampire was off the streets. The thought brought real tears to my eyes, as did the images of my mother, father, and brother.

Maciah's hold softened. "Are you hurt?"

"Just a few bruises and a sprained ankle," I replied.

"We're almost there."

Another minute later, Maciah slowed down. We were in an alley somewhere far from the bar. Him running was quicker for getting away than the Tesla we had to leave behind.

There were two vampires from Maciah's nest in the silver sedan as we got into the back seat.

"Everything okay?" the driver asked.

"It is. Head back to the house so we can go home," Maciah answered.

Home never sounded so good.

26

WITHIN THE HOUR, WE WERE ON THE PLANE AND HEADED back to Portland. After having Maciah's help removing the three pounds of makeup on my face and my ruined dress, I slept the rest of the flight back.

Maciah tried to carry me to the waiting SUV, but I stood up on my own and walked. I was still tired, but I wasn't hurting and we weren't on the run, so there was no reason to rush.

"Any news from the vampires driving home?" Nikki asked.

"No, but Beatrix somehow has my phone number and texted me. She said Rigo's men have no idea who we are, and they're searching LA for three women they'll never find," Maciah said.

While I was relieved to hear that, something didn't feel right. Everything had been too easy. Sure, I'd had the crap beaten out of me, but I still felt like the other shoe had yet to drop. Something had to go wrong. Life didn't often give without taking in return.

I kept my thoughts to myself, though. Everyone else seemed to be thrilled with how our plans went. Well, except for the part when I'd been behind closed doors, and they'd had no clue if I was alive or dead.

Maciah had kept those worries to himself once he had me in his arms. I was still blown away that he had let me handle things in the club. I'd thought for sure at some point that he'd attempt to be the typical man and interfere. As soon as we were alone, I'd have to show him my appreciation.

The SUV we'd taken to the airport was waiting for us in the parking lot and covered in snow. Thankfully, the runway had been cleared enough for us to land safely instead of being detoured to the main terminals.

Zeke began to clear the windows before getting into the driver's seat.

"I can't believe we only got two of them." Nikki sighed once we were all in the SUV.

"But Rigo was a big one. That will put a lot of them in hiding for a while, which means less humans dying or being turned," Rachel replied.

Her response made me wonder how hard it was going to be to get our chance at facing Dmitri. Given him and Rigo were from the same coven, would Dmitri stay hidden for longer? Or would he search for me until he found the one that took his pseudo-brother from him?

Either way, I'd make sure I was ready for him. If

Dmitri was smart enough to stay home and away from the party, then I doubted he would be irrational about Rigo's death. I was counting on the two of them being opposites.

We pulled through the gate at the mansion, and all of the lights were on. I knew vampires didn't need sleep, but normally they were resting at four in the morning. My guard instantly went up as I stared out the windshield.

"We should park up front instead of in the garage," I said.

Zeke shrugged, doing as I suggested.

"What's wrong?" Maciah asked me.

"I don't know. Maybe nothing, but don't you find it weird that so many lights are on?" I asked.

"The others are probably waiting up for us. They usually do that when we go out on missions like this," Maciah replied.

Oh. Well, that made sense. I was more on edge than I realized from earlier. A good night's sleep was probably all I needed.

"Want me to head into the garage, then?" Zeke asked before he turned the vehicle off.

"No. We'll take care of it later today. We've all had a long day." Maciah got out first, and I followed him. Zeke was already at the house by the time I came around the SUV.

I scanned the area as we approached. The scent of death was heavy in the air and there was blood dripping from the roses on the bush nearest to the front door.

The foreboding feeling I'd been holding on to ignited within my chest, but I was too late to warn anyone. Zeke had already stepped inside and there was a sword to his neck.

A man I'd never seen was standing just inside the doorway, holding Zeke hostage. "Welcome home, children."

Mother freaking Silas.

It had to be him. There was no one else I could think of that would call them "children." He pulled Zeke out of the entryway, keeping the sword at his throat, giving us a view of the many vampires inside the mansion that didn't belong.

"Come on in, and let's chat," Silas said. His voice was rough, as if he'd been punched in the throat one too many times.

He wore black cargo pants and a white t-shirt that was tight around his chest and arms, showing off muscles I didn't expect from a centuries-old vampire who was supposedly dying. His face had minimal wrinkles, and his dark blond hair showed no visible grays.

His dark red eyes roamed over me. "I can't believe you tried keeping her a secret, old friend."

"We were never friends," Maciah replied with a snarl, staying close to me.

Zeke was facing us, not at all scared that he could be dead at any moment. The sword was beginning to cut into his skin, beads of blood gathering on the silver blade, which also had to be burning him.

"You know, I had hoped you learned something from me during our time spent together, but the fact you left your home when you knew I was getting closer was such a disappointment. I'd brought my men here, promising them a fight, but there was little fuss as we took over your compound," Silas taunted.

"What do you want?" Maciah asked.

Silas chuckled. "Don't play ignorant with me, boy. Give me the girl, and I'll leave here with minimal damage. You can keep your precious home and lifestyle, and we'll never see each other again."

"I'll kill you before you get your hands on her," Maciah seethed.

Silas had us right where he wanted. Maciah could act like we had a leg to stand on, but there was no back-up coming anytime soon and Maciah couldn't actually kill Silas. Though, I could and that was tempting, but I didn't stand a chance against the horde of red-eyed vampires around us. None of Maciah's nest was anywhere to be seen.

"Well, then. That changes things." Silas slid the sword further into Zeke's throat, and blood spilled onto his shirt.

"Wait!" I called, stepping forward. I had one plan that could possibly save Zeke and the rest of us.

Silas paused. "Are you offering yourself up?"

I nodded, and Maciah pulled me back. "You can't do that, Amersyn."

My eyes met his, and I hated the fear held within his dark features.

"Trust me." I turned back to Silas, but stayed in Maciah's grasp. "You don't actually want me, right? You just want my blood."

The vampire shrugged. "Technically."

"If you take me, then you're going to have people after you. Not just Maciah, but others who are searching for me. I assume you're familiar with Viktor. You might not feel threatened by this nest, but Viktor could pose problems you don't need if you take what he's looking for. Wouldn't it be easier if you just took my blood and left us all alone?" I asked.

Silas considered my offer but didn't lessen his hold on Zeke, who was beginning to sag, causing more blood to spill from his open wound.

"I need a lot of blood, and if you fight me at any point, I will kill you and still take your blood," Silas said.

"You won't find any resistance from me." It's not like I wanted to die, but I knew that doing so wouldn't actually mean the end of my life, which made the thought of death a little easier to swallow. Even though I very much did not want to be a vampire, if that was what it took to save Zeke, then I'd choose to be one of them any day of the week.

These vampires had shown me true friendship in the time that I'd known them. They had given me a new purpose, and I was going to repay that.

"Amersyn," Maciah pleaded with me, but I refused

to meet his stare. He was afraid and rightfully so, but I needed to do this. Nobody had to die this way.

"Let me go, Maciah," I said, looking only at a smirking Silas.

"No." His hold on me tightened.

Steeling my resolve, I finally turned to Maciah. "You have to let me do this."

"Actually, I don't."

"You'd let them all die for me? Because that's what's going to happen otherwise." I didn't normally let my opponent know when they had the upper hand, but it was so clear here that there was no pretending differently.

"I'd let the whole world die for you, Amersyn."

His words were like a punch to my gut, but I didn't have a moment to revel in them.

Silas hissed. "Enough! Give me what I came here for, or the offer is off the table."

"Let me go," I said with conviction, staring at Maciah's furious and nearly black eyes.

His grip tightened for another second longer before he let out a heavy breath. As a leader, he knew I was right. Everything about my choice felt right, even if they were all willing to die. This was the better option.

"I'm not okay with this," Maciah finally said as he released me. There was so much hurt lacing his words, but that wasn't something I could analyze too deeply at the moment. We'd have to get our frustrations out after there weren't vampires trying to kill us.

After Maciah let go of me, I turned back to Silas.

"Send your men outside except for two to keep things even and Nikki will go wherever you're holding our vampires and make sure they're still alive. If you've killed them, the deal is dead."

Silas released Zeke, and he dropped to the ground at his feet. Rachel moved to grab him, but Silas pointed the sword at her. "Touch him and your head comes off."

She sneered at her creator, tears in her eyes and ready to fight for her friend, but I could already see Zeke's neck closing up. He was going to be okay.

"I need you to watch my back," I said, pulling her toward me and giving her something else to focus on.

She straightened and nodded, standing next to Maciah.

"The rest of your nest is out back. You'll find them... mostly okay," Silas said, and Nikki took off in a blur.

Rachel pulled her phone out a moment later. "Yeah." Pause. "All of them?" Then, she hung up and confirmed everyone was still alive.

I stepped to Silas, with Maciah and Rachel right behind me. I held out my wrist, because there was no way that psycho was getting near my neck.

"If I'm not taking you with me, then I need something to put your blood in," Silas said, stepping on Zeke's back as he tried to get up.

That was interesting. I would have thought he just needed to drink it. This was better, though. The bloodsucker's lips wouldn't have to stay on my skin.

Rachel disappeared and was back within a few

seconds. She threw a liter-sized glass bottle at him. "There."

Silas laughed. "Yeah, that's not going to be enough."

She hissed in return, leaving to go get more. I wasn't sure how much blood I could lose and not die, but hopefully Rachel knew from her nurse training and would only bring back enough containers to keep me under that threshold.

Silas grabbed my wrist as we waited, jerking me toward him and out of Maciah's reach.

Maciah moved to grab me back, but Silas had his sword up and pierced Maciah's chest. "Touch her and you're both dead."

Maciah snarled but stepped back just enough that the tip of the sword slid out of his chest. I hated this more than any of them would ever know.

I tried to pull away from Silas, but he was just as strong and powerful as Maciah had warned.

Rachel was back with three bottles the same size as the previous one, and I did my best not to show my concern at how much blood was going to be coming out of my body.

Silas's fangs tore into my wrist without notice, and I cried out. Maciah came toward me, but I held my other hand out to stop him, trying to breathe through the pain as the sinister vampire drank from me.

I grabbed Silas's long hair and jerked him up. "Take-out only, asshole."

My blood covered his lips, and he smirked at me. "I

just needed to test the goods first, but I'm glad to see you have some fight in you."

He still had the first bottle in his hand and turned my wrist until my blood began pouring into the glass. "You better hope that vein stays all the way open. Otherwise, we could be here all day," Silas added.

Evil freaking bastard.

After the first bottle was full, he grabbed another, smirking. "I might need to take another bite. The blood is slowing."

This would be the only time I wasn't glad to have accelerated healing.

Rachel handed me a silver dagger she must have had on her. Best friend ever.

Halfway through the second bottle, I cut my wrist with the silver blade. Given my heritage, I hoped that would keep the vein open longer than Silas's fangs.

By the time we were working on the fourth container, I was swaying and could no longer stand. Maciah brought me a chair since Silas didn't seem keen on leaving the front door, even though he still had two vampires behind him that had kept quiet, but on guard.

"Almost there." Silas was giddy.

His two vampires began picking up the bottles of my blood. I tried to watch every detail, but I couldn't hold my head up any longer.

Rachel was at my side, keeping me upright, and I could sense Maciah still behind me, hopefully keeping watch for anything else Silas might have been up to.

"All done. I'd say it's been a pleasure doing business

with you, but that would be a lie." Silas eyed my wrist, and I tried to hold it close to my chest, but I didn't have the strength to do so.

He leaned down, getting eye level with me. "We'll be seeing each other again, Amersyn."

Before I could respond, Silas and his vampires were gone.

Rachel carried me to the couch, and I wondered why it wasn't Maciah doing so. "I'm going to go get you some blood from the fridge." The horror must have shown on my face, because she elaborated. "I can give you an IV."

A blood transfusion. I could handle that.

Maciah and Zeke were speaking in hushed voices, then everything went quiet.

"Maciah?" I called weakly.

He stood above me, face hard and eyes dark with threads of crimson. "You have no idea what you've just done."

"I saved your nest." I'd known he was going to be upset with me, but I didn't expect his harsh tone.

"They would have gladly all died instead of letting that bastard have the power that's in your blood. You have no idea what Silas is going to be capable of now."

"We'll kill him. We'll get help, and everything—"

He cut me off. "No, Amersyn. We won't be doing anything. Not anymore."

"You've got to be kidding me! I almost just died to save Zeke and likely the rest of the vampires here. Silas hasn't done anything with my blood yet. We can go after him as soon as the others are back. I made the right choice."

Hadn't I? I didn't like that Maciah was making me second-guess myself, but unless he'd failed to tell me something—again—then I couldn't think of any reason for him to be so furious.

"You won't be able to kill Silas once that amount of your blood mixes with his. You will be his creator, Amersyn."

Yeah, that was something I should have known, but I wasn't going to be pissed at him for not knowing. We couldn't change what had already happened. We needed to work together. If I could see that now, why couldn't he?

Maciah turned without another word, disappearing from my line of sight, and there was nothing I could do as another wave of nausea rolled through me from the blood loss.

I knew without a shadow of doubt in my heart that Silas was going to die. I'd made the right choice, and we'd get another chance to end that vampire.

As I waited for Rachel to return, I began to plot how I was going to kill Silas, immortal or not. I just hoped Maciah could sort out the real reason he was so furious with me and be by my side when I finished what I'd started.

The story continues in Vampire Ash, releasing December 2021!
Want to read other books from the Mystics and Mayhem world while you wait? Check out Broken Court and Luna Marked next!

STAY IN TOUCH

Find Heather on Facebook:
Reader Group:
Want to talk all things books and get updates before
anyone else? Come hang with me in my reader group!
Heather Renee's Book Warriors

Author Page:
Teaser and big updates are also posted here!
Heather Renee Author

Newsletter:
I send this out sporadically. Don't worry. You won't
ever be spammed by me and you get a couple goodies
when you sign up!
http://smarturl.it/HeatherReneeNL

featuring wolves, witches, vengeance, and fated mates.

Blood of the Sea Series

A complete Young Adult Paranormal Romance series featuring vampires, open seas adventures, and the occasional pirate.

Standalone

Marked Paradox - A complete Young Adult Fantasy fae story about a realm divided and one fae to bring them back together.

ACKNOWLEDGMENTS

A big thank you to my husband and daughter for their continued support in making my dreams become a reality! I love you both so much!

As always, massive thanks to my editor and bestie Jamie Holmes. I love you long time!

Thank you to my assistant Michelle for your continued support. It means so much to me!

Lots of thanks to my cover designer Jay. I couldn't imagine publishing these books without your creative genius!

Another thank you to Brittney Proffit for naming the bar in this series: Crossroads. And thanks to Kimberley Richardson for naming the night club Nyx!

Lastly, thank you to my readers for your continued support! I'm so thankful to each and every one of you!

ABOUT THE AUTHOR

Heather Renee is a *USA Today* bestselling author who lives in Oregon. She writes urban fantasy and paranormal romance novels with a mixture of adventure, humor, and sass. Her love of reading eventually led to her passion for writing and giving the gift of escapism.

When Heather's not writing, she is spending time with her loving husband and beautiful daughter, going on their own adventures. For more ways to connect with her, visit www.HeatherReneeAuthor.com.

Lightning Source UK Ltd.
Milton Keynes UK
UKHW051826060223
416577UK00008B/605/J

9 781735 474663